THE EMPTY CABIN

The door was open. Not a crack, as it would be to let in fresh air, but standing wide enough for him to enter. It verified the Kendalls weren' t home. Lisa would never be so careless.

Nate scanned the interior. Immediately, to forestall being shot, he jerked back. Once again no shots rang out. Sucking in a deep breath, Nate drew his other pistol, then sprang inside, to the right of the doorway. He had a jumbled impression of objects being where they shouldn't, of a table that was supposed to be on the left now in the middle of the room, and of a chest of drawers that had been moved.

Waiting a full minute to confirm he was alone before he moved, Nate straightened and walked to the west window. As he recollected, the Kendalls kept a lantern on a peg close by. It wasn't there.

Nate gingerly felt his way to the fireplace. The logs had long since gone cold. Fishing his fire steel and flint from his possibles bag, he lit a small fire that soon blazed high. After adding more logs from the bin, he rose and turned.

His first impression had been all wrong. The furniture hadn't been moved around. It had been *thrown* every which way.

The *Wilderness* series:

#1: KING OF THE MOUNTAIN
#2: LURE OF THE WILD
#3: SAVAGE RENDEZVOUS
#4: BLOOD FURY
#5: TOMAHAWK REVENGE
#6: BLACK POWDER JUSTICE
#7: VENGEANCE TRAIL
#8: DEATH HUNT
#9: MOUNTAIN DEVIL
#10: BLACKFOOT MASSACRE
#11: NORTHWEST PASSAGE
#12: APACHE BLOOD
#13: MOUNTAIN MANHUNT
#14: TENDERFOOT
#15: WINTERKILL
#16: BLOOD TRUCE
#17: TRAPPER'S BLOOD
#18: MOUNTAIN CAT
#19: IRON WARRIOR
#20: WOLF PACK
#21: BLACK POWDER
#22: TRAIL'S END
#23: THE LOST VALLEY
#24: MOUNTAIN MADNESS
#25: FRONTIER MAYHEM
#26: SLAY GROUND
#27: GOLD RAGE

GIANT SPECIAL EDITIONS:

ORDEAL
HAWKEN FURY
SEASON OF THE WARRIOR
PRAIRIE BLOOD
THE TRAIL WEST
FRONTIER STRIKE
SPANISH SLAUGHTER

WILDERNESS

28

The Quest

David Thompson

LEISURE BOOKS  NEW YORK CITY

To Judy, Joshua, and Shane.

A LEISURE BOOK®

August 1999

Published by

Dorchester Publishing Co., Inc.
276 Fifth Avenue
New York, NY 10001

ISBN 0-8439-4572-9

Printed in the United States of America.

The Quest

Chapter One

The frantic rider did not see the beauty of the world around him. He did not see the sterling blue sky, the china white clouds. He paid no attention to the lush, virgin woodland through which he raced. Startled deer bounded from his path, but he never realized they were there. Smaller creatures, rabbits and chipmunks and squirrels, scattered at his thunderous approach, their presence ignored.

Part of the reason the man was blind to everything had to do with the tears streaming from his eyes. A greater part could be blamed on the raw terror that encased his hammering heart in an icy sheath. He was scared, this man. Scared to the depths of his soul. Scared not for himself but for others.

As the rider burst from the woodland and shot off across a grassy valley, he groaned. More a wail of abject despair, it wavered on the breeze like the spectral moan of a tormented spirit. Shaggy buffalo grazing nearby heard it and looked up in alarm. A huge bull snorted and pawed the ground, challenging the newcomer, but the distraught rider was rapidly rushing away and the bull saw no need to attack. It snorted again, grumbling as males of all stripe are wont to do when annoyed, and returned to feeding and eyeing a cow.

The rider never saw the buffalo. Had the bull been a grizzly, the man would have been in dire peril. Under his breath he said to himself, "No! No! No!" Only he knew why, although the tears and the fear lining his features were a clue.

Buckskins clothed the rider's rugged frame. Like most of his hardy breed, he had a powder horn and ammo pouch slung crosswise across his chest. Slung over his back was a heavy Hawken, which jounced and swayed with the motion of the sorrel.

Ahead a creek appeared. Beside it, on a low bank, stood a tidy cabin with a small flower garden in front. As the rider neared the homestead, the front door opened and out strolled a young woman in a homespun dress, carrying an empty basket. She heard him and whirled, fearing hostiles. Recognizing her visitor, she smiled and waved and called out, "Scott! This is a surprise! What brings you—"

The woman stopped. She saw the tears and his expression. "Scott? What is it? What's wrong?"

He was well within earshot, but he did not reply. Instead, he sped on around the rear of the cabin without so much as a glance in her direction. The young woman took a few quick steps, hiking an arm.

"Scott? Please! What's the matter? Simon will be home soon! We can help, whatever it is!"

Her words, or her yell, registered. The rider raised his head and shouted, "Nate! Need Nate!" And with that he galloped on across the valley, leaving a cloud of dust and a mystified woman in his wake.

No sooner had the man shouted than he shut everything from his mind except the task he had set for himself, a task that meant the difference between life and death for the two people he most adored. Under his breath again he repeated the name, "Nate! Nate! Nate!" in a tortured tone, as if it were his sole hope of salvation. And in a very real sense, it was.

"Please be there!" the rider declared, and sniffled. He blinked to shed the tears, but new ones welled up to replace those trickling down his ruddy cheeks.

"Please be there!"

Life was good.

Or so Nate King decided as he swung his ax in a glittering arc. The keen edge sliced into the branch on the ground in front of him, cleaving the pine cleanly. Beside him was a pile of freshly chopped firewood that rose as high as his waist. A big pile, because Nate King was a big man. Tall, broad-shouldered, wide of chest and narrow of hip, his powerful physique radiated strength and vitality like the sun radiated heat and light.

Nate was on a knoll not far from the family's cabin. Down at the lake his son and his son's betrothed were fishing. In a field to the north his wife and small daughter were gathering roots. It was a tranquil scene, the lake a pristine blue, their remote high-country valley ringed by majestic peaks crowned by glistening snow. Their "private paradise," was how Nate liked to think of it.

At moments like these, when all was right with the world, when his family was in good health and everyone was happy and enjoying rare moments of pure leisure, Nate was supremely content. "It doesn't get any better than this," he commented aloud.

The bay tethered a few yards away nickered and stamped a hoof. Nate chuckled, shaking his head, and said, "No. I'm not done yet. Be patient."

Nate had been chopping wood for most of the morning, a chore he relished. Stripped to the waist, he was caked with sweat, his raven hair matted. Now he wiped a brawny hand across his brow and hefted the ax anew. Another half an hour and he would be done. Tomorrow or the next day he would add the pile to the small mountain of firewood close to the cabin, enough to last them most of the winter unless it was particularly severe.

Some folks might think it silly of Nate to cut wood in the middle of the summer. But in the wilderness it wasn't smart to leave any job to the last minute. Laziness was a luxury only those who lived in cities dared indulge. In the wilds it was equivalent to certain death. The man who failed to plan ahead never lived long enough to plan anything.

By autumn Nate had to have enough wood, jerky, pemmican, and other essentials stocked to see his family through to spring. So here he was, in ninety-degree heat, burying the ax in another downed limb. He liked the sensation, the feel of the smooth handle, the ripple of his muscles, the cool layer of perspiration. And it was great exercise.

Although close to twenty years had gone by since Nate left the hustle and bustle of New York City for the Rocky Mountains, he still remembered how life there had been. How men and women spent most of their waking hours at jobs where their only exercise was scribbling with quill pens. How lacing their shoes or boots was the most strenuous thing they did all day. As a result they grew overweight and sluggish, sort of like bears about to den up for the winter. They had more fat than sinew, and the simple act of walking around the block left them puffing for breath.

In the wilds it was different. Those who were out of shape paid for their sloth with their lives. The creatures who were plumpest were the first to be preyed upon.

To survive, a man must always be alert, always mentally sharp, always at his best. His reflexes had to be honed to a razor's edge. Thankfully, Nate was kept so busy from dawn to dusk, month in and month out, that becoming a sluggard was the least of his concerns. Constant activity had hardened his muscles to a steely temper. His stomach was solid rock, his chest, his shoulders corded tight. And his senses were as sharp as those of a bird of prey or a panther.

So it was that the faintest of sounds brought his chin up a second time. Swiveling, Nate scoured a high ridge to the south. He cocked his head and listened intently. The bay's ears pricked, confirming that the muted pounding he heard wasn't his imagination.

Nate leaned the ax against a pine and retrieved his Hawken. His pistols lay on his buckskin shirt, along with his possibles bag. Letting them lie there for the moment, he stepped to the left for a clearer view of the ridge. Whoever was coming up the other side had to be either a skilled horseman or a lunatic. Both slopes were treacherously steep and littered with talus. Anyone who tried to go up and over was taking their life into their hands.

Wreathed by a shimmering halo of dust, a rider materialized on the crest. The man flew on down without a moment's hesitation, and the instant his mount hit the incline they were in trouble. Talus spewed out from under the horse. It tried to steady itself by bracing its forelegs but trying to stay upright on a sliding layer of loose earth and stones was like trying to walk on greased glass. It couldn't be done.

Nate saw the rider haul on the reins and seek to veer to the left, but it was too late. The horse tossed its head and pumped, tilting as momentum and gravity got the better of it. More dust billowed skyward.

The rider was practically standing in the stirrups, doing all he could to keep the animal erect. Even at that distance Nate heard its squeal of terror. Both were almost horizontal, the man straining with all his might to avoid the inevitable. In a violent spray of dirt and rocks they crashed onto their sides and were swept downward like twigs caught in the grip of an avalanche. The man was sent flying from the saddle to roll like tumbleweed as loud rumbling echoed off surrounding peaks.

Even before the talus came to a stop, Nate King was in

motion. He spun and ran to the two pistols. His loved ones had stopped what they were doing and were gazing toward the ridge. He fired first one flintlock into the ground, then the other, and at the signal his wife and son headed for the cabin at a run. Wedging the pistols under his wide brown leather belt, he swiftly donned his shirt and bounded to the bay.

The slope below the ridge was largely still except for random rolling stones and shifting currents of dirt. At the bottom was a high mound, tendrils of dust rising like so much smoke. Of the rider and his mount there was no sign.

Nate galloped southward, dreading the worst. There was something about the rider that was vaguely familiar. The man had been too far off to note facial details, but obviously it was a white man. Few Indians used saddles. Nate weaved into a belt of firs, losing sight of the ridge for the time being.

A strong urge to stop and reload both pistols came over him, which was understandable. One of the most important lessons a frontiersman learned, often at great cost, was to *never, ever* venture anywhere with unloaded guns. To do so was to court death; too many menaces lurked in the shadowed glens and murky forest depths.

When Zach was younger, Nate had spent months impressing on the boy that as soon as he fired a rifle or pistol he must immediately reload. Now here Nate was, violating the most basic of wilderness tenets. But Nate felt that if he didn't, that if he delayed reaching the slope by even a few minutes, the delay would result in the rider's death. Provided he wasn't already dead.

Nate hoped he was wrong, that when he emerged from the trees the rider would be on his feet. It was the horse, though, he spotted first. An exhausted, badly bruised and severely shaken sorrel, stumbling among the littered debris. There was still no trace of the man. Nate reined up at the base, where the dust was thick enough to choke on. Vaulting down, he swatted at the gleaming particles and climbed, the footing treacherous, the talus sliding out from under his moccasins with every step. Much like shifting quicksand, it threatened to suck him in or pitch him off balance.

Suddenly Nate halted and glanced at the sorrel. He knew that horse! "Scott?" he called out. "Scott Kendall? Can you hear me?"

Silence mocked him, punctuated by the rattle of small rocks and the hiss of loose dirt. Natc forged higher, wary of spots that oozed like watery rivulets. A low rumble from above caused him to stiffen. One slide might easily trigger another, and if that happened, he'd be caught in the path of tons of hurtling earth.

Seconds later the rumbling stopped. Using the Hawken for extra support, Nate continued higher. He hollered Kendall's name over and over, but the man didn't answer.

Nate hated to think his friend was dead. They had met before Nate's daughter was born, and now she was almost nine. Many an evening they had sat around campfires in the high country or at tables in their respective cabins swapping tall tales over steaming cups of coffee or glasses of whiskey. They shared a special bond born of hardships overcome and dangers defeated.

Sweeping his gaze from right to left, Nate was about to go higher still when a crooked object caught his eye. It jutted from the talus like a busted branch. It was a leg clothed in torn buckskin, bent limply at the knee. Darting toward it, Nate nearly lost his footing when the section of talus on which he stood abruptly streamed down. Flinging himself onto a patch of stable stones, he crouched and waited for the movement around him to cease. Every second was precious, and he chafed at the delay, but it couldn't be helped.

At last the talus settled. Nate hurried on, treading lightly, gingerly, as if on eggshells. Kendall's leg hadn't moved, a bad omen. Reaching it, Nate set the Hawken down. His friend's other foot was visible, barely enough for him to latch a firm grip with both hands and pull. Slowly, resisting mightily, the other leg appeared, and once it did, Nate gripped both, steadied himself, and heaved backward.

The strain was tremendous. It felt as if Scott Kendall weighed a ton. Nate bunched his shoulders and tried again. He succeeded in pulling Kendall halfway out, but no farther.

Gritting his teeth, Nate braced himself for another try and threw all his weight and strength into the effort. With excruciating slowness Kendall's body rose higher, steadily higher. Nate was making headway, but his friend had been without air for minutes and must surely have suffocated.

Nate rocked back on his heels, challenged to his limit, the veins on his temples bulging in stark relief. "Come on!" he fumed, tugging and wrenching. The body rose some more, past the waist to the chest. Then it stuck fast and wouldn't budge.

"Damn it!" Nate said, refusing to be beaten. Hunkering, he wrapped his arms around Kendall's hips, clamped hold, and surged upward as if striving to uproot a tree by sheer brute force. For terrible moments it appeared Nate had failed. The body refused to yield—until, with a jolt, it popped from the talus like a cork popping from a bottle and Nate was thrown onto his rump. Quickly, he scrambled to Kendall's side and bent low. As he'd dreaded, his friend wasn't breathing.

"No!" Nate placed both hands flat on the other's stomach and pushed in deep, a trick he had seen used by a Shoshone on a child that nearly drowned in the Green River. But nothing happened. He pushed again, and a third time. Had he been too late? Was all this in vain? He pumped madly, not knowing what else to do.

Scott Kendall was pale, his face covered with grime, his reddish beard caked with dirt. A wide gash above the left ear bled profusely. He was a big man in his own right, heavy with muscle. On a few occasions, at the annual rendezvous, they had wrestled, and Nate had been impressed by his friend's bulk and weight. Now both worked against them, preventing him from saving Scott's life.

Unwilling to be denied, Nate put his hands on Kendall's chest, one on top of the other, and in desperation resumed pumping. He had no idea whether it would do any good. He just wanted to get Kendall's lungs working again. Push-stop-push-stop-push-stop. Repeatedly, Nate performed the same driving thrust. His arms were tiring and sweat was dripping from his chin when, unexpectedly, Scott Kendall lurched convulsively and coughed.

Nate pumped again, but there was no need. His friend was heaving and sputtering and wheezing like a blacksmith's bellows. Nate sat back, weary but elated, as the other mountaineer sucked in air. In a while Kendall's breathing became normal. But to Nate's dismay, he didn't open his eyes or sit up.

"Scott?"

Rousing himself, Nate rose onto his knees and shook Kendall's shoulder. Scott's eyelids fluttered, but otherwise there was no reaction. Nate shook him again, harder. *Now what?* he thought, and examined the head wound. It was worse than he had guessed, deeper and jagged, caused by the most severe of blows. No wonder Kendall was still out to the world.

Rising, Nate claimed the Hawken, then bent and lifted his friend. He figured that he could make it down without too much difficulty, but he figured wrong. His first stride nearly resulted in disaster. Talus slid out from under him so fast, he pitched forward and would have fallen except for a large boulder that resisted the pull of the earthen mercury and enabled him to check his plunge by propping a foot against it.

How else can we get down? Nate wondered, and received his answer in the form of crackling brush and the sudden appearance of his son and the young woman his son was engaged to. "Zach! Louisa! I need your help!"

Zachary King was all of seventeen years old. He had his father's black hair and green eyes, and like his father he favored buckskins. But his were fashioned more in true Shoshone style, and his hair was worn as a Shoshone would wear it. His knife sheath, his moccasins, were Shoshone. Unless given a close scrutiny, he could easily pass for a full-blooded warrior. Springing from his dun, he hastened to the talus.

Beside the young man ran the girl Zach loved. Louisa May Clark was only sixteen, but by frontier standards that made her a woman. She was old enough to marry, old enough to bear children. Indeed, girls who had not wed by her age were branded peculiar. By twenty, unwed females were considered old maids.

But Louisa Clark hadn't accepted Zach's proposal out of fear of becoming a spinster. She loved him, loved him dearly, loved him as she had loved only two other people in her whole life: her mother and father. She'd lost the former on their arduous trek across the vast prairie. Her father had later been slain by hostiles. Now she was on her own—or had been until she met the one who had claimed her heart.

"What do you want us to do, Pa?" Zach asked. They were a good fifty feet below where his father stood.

"Do you have your tomahawk?" Nate responded.

Zach pointed at a parfleche draped over the dun, behind the saddle. "In there."

"Chop down three straight limbs about seven feet long. Trim off the shoots and leaves and bring them here. As fast as you can."

Zachary turned, but Lou beat him to the dun and unfastened the flap with a deft twirl of her fingers. The tomahawk was on top. Zach accepted it and led her into the trees, scanning high and low for suitable branches. He found one on the ground, another low on a wide pine. The last was beside a log. "These should do us."

"What does your pa have in mind?"

"I don't rightly know. But he wants them, so he gets them."

Louisa couldn't get over how close-knit the Kings were, how deeply they trusted and relied on one another. Back in the States, many families had honed bickering to a fine art and spent more time squabbling than sharing. Not so the Kings. They treated each other with a degree of respect rare to behold. And they were always ready to lend one another a helping hand, unlike her own relatives, who could only be persuaded to help out when it was in their best interests.

Drawing her knife, Lou helped trim. As she worked, she studied her sweetheart on the sly, admiring how his lean body flowed with each swing of the tomahawk. She never tired of gazing at him. He was the single most handsome male in all Creation. Or so she believed, and woe to anyone who sought to convince her differently.

Zach King was thinking about the man his father was helping. He'd glimpsed Kendall's face, and was curious why the man had shown up so early. The two families weren't slated to get together for another moon.

Up on the talus, Nate hollered for them to hurry. He wanted to get his friend to his wife without delay. Winona was a highly skilled healer, her knowledge of herbal cures remarkable. She could gauge better than he how serious the wound was, and what was needed to mend it.

"Bring the last one," Zach said to Lou while dragging two of the limbs off. He had a fair notion what his pa had in mind. When he came to the talus he ascended without being told.

Nate had set Scott down so he could palm his butcher knife and cut a strip from the bottom of his shirt to use as a makeshift bandage, which did little to staunch the flow of blood. Now he began to cut whangs from under his arms and give them to his son. "Tie them together in pairs," he directed.

The fringe on their outfits served a variety of purposes. It helped drain rainwater off so the seams wouldn't swell. It reduced the wear and tear on their elbows and forearms. And best of all, the long strips could be cut off and used as binding.

In this case, Nate planned to use them to keep Kendall from slipping off the poles. He laid the long limbs side by side, about a foot apart. Then, with Zach's help, he placed their friend on top and lashed Scott's wrists and ankles to the outer ones.

"You sure this will work, Pa?"

"No," Nate admitted. If anything went wrong, Kendall could wind up worse off than he already was. "The two of you take the top. I'll take the bottom." So saying, Nate slid lower, slinging the Hawken over a shoulder. He lashed the three lower ends as closely together as he could, then gripped the outer limbs. "Ready?" Working together was essential, otherwise the crude travois would fall apart.

Zach nodded.

"Whenever you are," Lou said, praying she wouldn't mess up. Ever since she arrived at their cabin, she had been doing her utmost to show Zach's folks she was worthy of being a King. She did all she could to help out his ma; she treated little Evelyn as the sister she'd never had; and when given a chore, she did it to the absolute best of her ability.

The Kings didn't demand such perfection. They were relaxed and easygoing. No, Lou imposed it on herself. She couldn't shake the feeling that she was an outsider, that she must prove herself to them in order to be fully accepted. Silly, she knew, but that was how she felt, and she could no more discard her feelings than she could stop breathing.

"On the count of three," Nate said, and counted. On

"three," he lifted the ends and backed slowly down the slope. The poles slid loosely on the talus, carrying Kendall with them. Zach and Lou insured that the top ends didn't drift wide, Lou placing her hands on either side of the trapper's head so it wouldn't drag.

"Easy does it," Nate instructed.

The fifty feet seemed like five hundred. They had to stop often so Nate could set down his end and push large rocks out of the way or roll small boulders aside. More times than Nate cared to count the talus started to give way, the dirt caving in on itself and stopping only when they stood stock-still.

"Where do you reckon his wife and daughter are?" Lou asked Zach. She'd enjoyed their company when the two families got together. Lisa, the mother, was a naturally friendly soul, always in fine spirits. Vail Marie, the little daughter, was a bundle of energy who kept her parents hopping to keep up with her. "I hope they're safe. I like them."

"I hope so too," Zach replied. He liked the Kendalls also—liked them a lot—in large part because they treated him no differently than they treated everyone else. Not all whites did. Too many of his father's kind looked down their noses at him because he was of mixed blood, half white, half Shoshone—a half-breed. And as he had learned through bitter experience, 'breeds were generally despised by whites and Indians alike, a state of affairs that angered him whenever such rank bigotry reared its ugly head.

"Don't let your end slip," Nate cautioned. He was thinking ahead, to how they could get Kendall to their cabin without jostling him. A sturdier travois would suffice but would take most of an hour to rig—and they didn't have an hour to spare.

Lou stared at the blood on Scott Kendall's head. It had stained the bandage and continued to dampen his hair and beard. She recollected her pa telling her that if a person lost too much blood, they died. It was plain they must do something soon to stop the bleeding or the poor man wouldn't live out the day.

If there was any one aspect to life in the mountains that Lou disliked most, it was the violence. Violent accidents. Violent enemies. The raw violence of Nature itself. She never felt completely safe, as she did back in the States, because she never knew from one moment to the next when a new threat would arise.

As if on cue, Nate King stopped and gazed past them, above the talus. "Hold up. Don't make any sudden moves."

Lou hated to look, but she had to. Slowly turning her head, she spied the one creature that was more than a match for her prospective father-in-law. How could she miss it when it rivaled a bull buffalo in size? "Dear Lord, no," she breathed.

The grizzly on top of the ridge growled.

Chapter Two

Louisa May Clark had known the King family a relatively short time. Yet in that brief span she had come to regard them as rather remarkable. Besides being so close-knit and considerate of one another, they were some of the bravest people she'd ever met. She was given another example of their courage as the grizzly started down the slope toward them. Did either Nate or Zach show the slightest fear? They did not. They faced the monster as calmly as she would a stray dog, acting as if it were nothing to get excited about, as if having a grizzly interested in devouring them was the most normal occurrence on the face of the earth. Her future father-in-law seemed more annoyed than anything else. Unslinging his Hawken, he sidled to the right for a clear shot, careful not to dislodge the talus.

Zach had put himself between her and the bear, an act that endeared him to her all the more. He was so protective. When they first met it had bothered her some. She was a grown girl. She could take care of herself. But then she realized he was doing it out of love, not out of any urge to run roughshod over her, and she had come to accept his protectiveness. She imagined that when they were married he would do the same, but she wouldn't mind as long as he didn't turn into one of those men who treated their wives like helpless babies, as some friends of her pa had done.

At that moment, unknown to her, Zach King was regretting that Lou had tagged along. He'd wanted to leave her at the cabin with his mother and sister, but she insisted on coming and he couldn't bring himself to refuse. Things would change once they were man and wife. Then he could speak more freely, and he would be damned if he would let any wife of his put herself in harm's way. For their mutual peace of mind, once they had their own place it would be best if she stayed close to home.

Nate King pressed his Hawken to his shoulder but didn't fire. At that range he'd only wound the beast, and a wounded grizzly was a ferocious demon, unstoppable unless struck in a vital organ. Which was hard to do, thanks to their thick skulls and hides. As Lewis and Clark had learned on their famous expedition, dropping a griz took grit, perseverance, and plenty of ammunition.

The bear halted short of the upper edge of the talus field. It sniffed suspiciously, perhaps disturbed by lingering dust. Its enormous head swung from side to side as if the bear were seeking a safe way down. Apparently it had dealings with talus before.

Nate wasn't worried—yet. He'd slain more than his share of the great bears. When he initially came to the Rockies, the mountains literally crawled with them, and every other month or so he'd been pitted in combat with one. It had earned him a name unique among whites. To the Shoshones and the Crows, the Flatheads and the Utes, the Cheyennes and Arapahos, he was known as Grizzly Killer.

As the years went by, as more and more trappers flocked to the mountains, the number of silvertips along the foothills and the lower slopes dwindled. But those in the high alpine regions of the Rockies were as numerous and formidable as ever.

Nate sighted along the Hawken. The grizzly was prowling to the left, nose low to the soil. Nate speculated it was trying to pick up their scent in the mistaken belief it could descend the same way they had. Little did it know. He saw the brute start onto the talus, then draw up short when its paws dislodged a torrent. Backpedaling, it regained solid footing and snorted in irritation.

"Want me to fire a shot to try and scare it off?" Zach asked. He was well aware that grizzlies were fearless, but he didn't want the bear getting any closer, not with Lou present.

"No, Stalking Coyote," Nate said, using Zach's Shoshone name.

"Maybe it will just go away," Louisa said.

Zach almost laughed out loud. Grizzlies never gave up. The idea was ridiculous, but he didn't say so to Lou for fear of offending her. Quite a bit of late he found himself choking down words he might otherwise say, just to spare her feelings, and he took it for granted that was normal when two people were in love.

Rumbling deep in its huge barrel chest, the grizzly had climbed to the crest and was gazing at them. Silhouetted against the sky, it appeared almost regal—yet incredibly sinister. Turning, it shambled off down the other side.

"See?" Lou said happily. "What did I tell you? We're safe now."

Are we? Nate asked himself, and reslung the Hawken over his right shoulder. "Work fast," he commanded, bending to the poles. Acutely conscious of every passing second, he resumed their descent, moving with less care than before, anxious to reach the bottom. So anxious that when dirt slid from under him he didn't stop.

Louisa sensed the mountain man's urgency and divined the reason. She checked behind them several times, but the grizzly hadn't reappeared. Nate was unduly concerned, she reflected. They weren't in any danger. Why would the bear go to all the trouble to travel completely around the ridge?

It was the blood, Nate was thinking. Kendall's freshly spilled blood. The grizzly had caught a whiff of it, and the monster's bestial instincts had been inflamed. Their only hope to avoid a possibly fatal clash was to mount up and get out of there before the silvertip returned.

One of the horses whinnied. All four had their ears erect and were fidgeting nervously, Lou's mare worst of all. The bay was staring at the west end of the ridge, two hundred yards away.

"What's got them so skittish?" Louisa asked, the answer occurring to her the moment the words were out of her mouth. "Oh," she said, and felt foolish. "It's going to come after us, isn't it?"

"Yes," Zach said. He knew they would be lucky to escape unharmed. A grizzly's ferocity and cunning were matched only by its single-minded determination in pursuit of prey. Once a bear began a stalk, it didn't like to quit until its fangs were buried in its quarry.

A low roar from the west end of the ridge was added incentive for them to hurry. Nate reckoned it was a young bruin; an older grizzly would know better than to let them know where it was. He kicked a large rock from his path, avoided an eddy of swirling dirt, and drew within a dozen yards of the bottom.

"It'll be awful close, Pa," Zach said.

"What will?" Louisa asked.

Zach didn't answer. He was surprised she didn't realize their plight. Granted, she had little wilderness savvy, but he would hope his wife-to-be was sharp enough to think things through for herself. Not that he would adore her any less. Still—

Nate went a little too fast and paid for his mistake by having his moccasins wrenched out from under him. He fell onto his knees, pain searing up his thighs to his lower back. Undaunted, he shoved erect, firmed his grip, and partially walked, partially slid, the final few feet.

The whole while, Scott Kendall never stirred. His breathing was regular but shallow, half his face caked with drying blood.

Nate saw that his son and Lou were winded. He could use a short breather himself, but an overriding sense of urgency spurred him into moving toward the horses without setting the travois down. "We'll throw Scott over the sorrel," he announced.

"Oh, God!" Lou exclaimed.

The bear was at the far end of the ridge. It stared for only a moment, then broke into a shuffling trot, moving with amazing swiftness for so large an animal. Its bulk was deceptive. At top speed, a grizzly could overtake a horse.

Pure fright gushed through Lou. She had to will her arms and legs to work, to help Stalking Coyote and his father lift Kendall and ease him onto the saddle, belly down. It took valuable seconds, seconds in which the bear drew rapidly nearer. When next she looked, the grizzly had slashed the distance by half. Another hundred yards and it would be on top of them. Lou's fright grew worse, nearly paralyzing her.

"Light a shuck!" Nate declared, pushing both of them toward their respective mounts. "Zach, you lead the sorrel." Without waiting to see if they obeyed, Nate sprang onto the bay, hauled on the reins, and did the last thing any sane person would do. He rode *toward* the grizzly instead of away from it.

"What's your pa doing?" Louisa asked, aghast, as she reached for her saddle horn.

"Saving our lives." Zach was already astride his dun. "Don't dawdle or we're goners!"

Lou didn't like his tone, but she climbed on and followed as he wheeled and trotted off. Within seconds they were in among the pines, and she felt a bit safer. At least the bear couldn't see them.

Nate King didn't resort to his Hawken. At a full gallop he

bore down on the grizzly, which never slackened speed. Gaping jaws wide, slavering with bloodlust, it was almost upon him when Nate swerved, flying past almost within reach of its paws. As he went by, he uttered a Shoshone whoop. The ruse succeeded. The bear forgot all about Zach and Louisa and came after him.

Nate had counted on luring the bear away. What he hadn't counted on was its uncanny quickness. It was on him within heartbeats, its forepaws raking the bay's tail, nearly shredding its flanks. The bay spurted forward, nickering, and from then on they were in a race for their lives with bristling death at their heels.

The griz gnashed empty air, eager to bring them down. Its claws clipped the bay's tail again.

Nate risked one quick glance to be sure Zach and Lou were gone, then he cut to the left, toward the ridge. When the bear did likewise, Nate reversed direction, angling toward the firs. It bought him a few extra yards, yards that might mean the difference between seeing his wife again and being turned into worm food. Bent low, he streaked into the woods without any regard for his safety. A low limb nearly took his head off. Another gouged his shoulder, almost unseating him.

Plowing through the undergrowth as if it didn't exist, the grizzly glued itself to the bay. It sounded like a steam engine about to explode, its paws thudding like the beat of a Cheyenne drum.

A narrow opening between a pair of saplings gave Nate an idea. Reining sharply, he sped between them with barely enough room to spare. He thought the barrier would slow the grizzly down, but he was wrong. They hardly gave it pause. The bear slammed into them with the force of a battering ram, snapping both as if they were dry twigs.

A log hove into sight, and Nate made straight for it. The bay, well trained, sailed up and over without breaking stride. To Nate's chagrin, the griz did the same, displaying astounding agility. It was a vivid demonstration, as if any were needed, of why so many trappers and Indians had lost their lives to the lords of the Rockies; they underestimated what the behemoths were capable of.

Nate had suffered from the same flaw when he was still green behind the ears. Back then there had been so much for him to learn. That mountain lions could leap twenty feet from a standing start. That buffalo would stampede at the click of a rifle hammer. That wolverines deserved their reputations for wanton savagery. That grizzlies were harder to kill than all of them combined.

Swiveling, Nate considered putting a ball into the beast's head. It might slow the silvertip long enough for him to escape.

A thicket loomed, half an acre of dense brush. Ordinarily Nate would give it a wide berth to spare the bay from scratches and scrapes. But now he plunged on in, lashing the reins, and true to form the grizzly barreled in after him. Nate slanted to one side, then the other. Each time he gained a few critical feet on his adversary, who wasn't adept at adapting to abrupt changes in direction. And, too, the bear had slowed a trifle to spare its eyes from the scores of thin limbs the bay broke, the tips thrusting like needles at its face.

Exploding into the open, Nate bore due west, leading the grizzly away from the cabin, away from his family. It surprised him the brute wasn't flagging yet. While silvertips were fast when they needed to be, they lacked endurance. After a quarter of a mile or so they tired and could run no farther.

Not this one. Snarling hideously, it sought to regain the ground it had lost. Its long, thick claws sheared at the bay's legs. It seemed that nothing short of the grizzly's death would stop it.

Nate racked his brain for a means of escaping in one piece. Grabbing hold of his bouncing powder horn, he did his best to hold it steady while opening it, then upended the horn over his other palm. Half the powder spilled onto his legs and saddle, but he clenched a handful and swiveled.

The grizzly was going all out, its mouth wider than ever, sucking air into its heaving lungs. Its massive wedge-shaped head rose, and it locked baleful eyes on him.

"Have a taste," Nate said, and flung the black powder. Some missed. More got into the bear's mouth and eyes. The hairy colossus snapped its jaws several times, then shook its head as if it had taken a bite of something it didn't like. "Like it?" Nate taunted, and threw another handful. Black powder wasn't toxic and wouldn't do more than give the brute a mild bellyache, but it tasted positively awful. And when it got in the eyes, it stung worse than salt.

Nate hurled a third handful, hoping his gamble paid off. He had used up most of his powder—and he had only the one shot in the Hawken. If the bear caught him he wouldn't last five seconds. A Green River knife was no match for over a thousand pounds of unbridled brawn and a bristling arsenal of teeth and claws.

The bear was snorting as if it had a cork stuck up its nose. It slowed and tossed its head, and for a few moments Nate believed his ploy had worked. Then the grizzly roared and came at him with renewed fury.

"You're pacing, Ma. Are you worried?"

Winona King halted in midstride and glanced at her daughter, seated on the edge of the bed against the wall. "No," she fibbed, and felt guilty doing so. It was not the Shoshone way to lie. But she wanted to spare her daughter needless anxiety. In truth, Winona was worried enough for both of them.

Evelyn wasn't fooled. "Ah, don't fret. Whatever it is, Pa can handle it. What can hurt him?"

Many things, Winona thought to herself. Her husband was stronger than most and wiser than many, but he wasn't invincible, their offspring's confidence notwithstanding. Winona had to remind herself it was normal for children to believe their parents could— What was that expression the whites used? Oh, yes. It was normal for children to believe their parents could walk on water. To someone of Evelyn's tender years, a parent was all-knowing and all-powerful. One of the greatest shocks a child experienced was to learn their mother and father were only human.

"I wish I could have gone with Zach and Lou," Evelyn mentioned. Like Winona, she wore a buckskin dress lavishly decorated with beads and red fringe her mother had traded for at Bent's Fort. Her hair was as black as Winona's but cut shorter, shoulder-length. Eyes sparkling, Evelyn hopped down and came to the doorway. "You'll wear a rut in the floor."

Despite herself, Winona laughed. Her daughter was developing a fine sense of humor. Winona took pride in how both of her children were turning out—but it hadn't always been so. Before Louisa came along, Winona had been deeply worried about Stalking Coyote. The hatred the boy had endured due to his mixed lineage had spawned bitter resentment, resentment she'd been afraid would one day erupt in violence if her son didn't learn to deal with it maturely.

"Did you hear something, Ma?" Evelyn asked.

"What?" Winona had been too deep in thought. Opening the door, she stepped outside, her hands resting on the flintlocks tucked under her beaded belt.

Evelyn rose onto her toes and screened her eyes with a hand. "I don't see them anywhere."

"Too many trees," Winona said.

"Do you think it's a war party?"

"I don't know."

"It could be Utes, but they're friendly now, aren't they? Maybe it's those mean old Bloods again."

"I don't—"

"Or the Blackfeet. They're still mad at Pa over that

fight up on the Yellowstone. Reckon they tried to sneak up on us?"

"I—"

"Or maybe it's some bad whites, like the ones who tried to make wolf meat of all of us a while ago. You don't think some of their kin have hunted us down, do you, Ma?"

Winona inwardly counted to ten. As dearly as she adored her daughter, there were times when Blue Flower tried her patience. Ever since the girl was old enough to talk, she had been one giant question mark. "We'll have to wait and find out."

"We could saddle up and go have a look-see. I'll even bring the horses around while you fetch your rifle."

"So that's what this was leading up to." Winona sighed. Her children had a devious streak she liked to say came from their father, but the fact of the matter was that her husband didn't have a deceitful bone in his handsome body. Nate was too forthright and honorable for his own good sometimes. Winona, however, was quite crafty, a trait she came by honestly. From an early age Shoshone girls were taught to hone their wits, both for dealing with men and for surviving in a world where nearly every other tribe considered them an enemy.

"Aw, shucks, Ma." Evelyn wasn't pleased. "I can't wait until I'm old enough to do as I want. Like Lou. She comes and goes as she sees fit. She gets to stay up late like the rest of you. When I'm sixteen I'll do the same."

"You will not."

"How's that, Ma?"

"So long as you live in this cabin, you will respect our wishes. Louisa has more freedom because she isn't our daughter. She won't be part of the family until she marries your brother, and then she'll be his wife and will be treated like every other adult."

Evelyn scratched her head. "She gets to do as she wants because she isn't your daughter, and I *don't* get to do as I want because I am?"

"Yes. Exactly."

"That's not fair."

"Life isn't fair. It never treats two people the same. One person might enjoy many years of health and happiness, another might be torn apart by a cougar at an early age."

"Why is that?" Evelyn's brow knit. "Remember last week when Pa was reading from the Bible? He said that God loves all of us. So how can God let one person be so happy and have the other suffer?"

Winona hesitated. To her people, the ways of the Great Mystery were just that—a mystery no one could penetrate. She recalled how amazed she had been when Nate showed her the white man's holy book. Whites had always struck her as bold, even arrogant, but never in her wildest imaginings would she think they were arrogant enough to put God on paper. After Nate taught her to read, she had studied the holy book and seen that her judgment had been hasty. Some parts of it she didn't quite comprehend, but other parts were ripe with beauty and insight.

"How can he?" Evelyn pressed her.

"Bad things happen to good people all the time," Winona began, and was interrupted again, although not by her daughter. From out of the woods trotted her son and Louisa, leading a third horse over which a body had been thrown.

Fearing it was the man who had claimed her heart, Winona dashed forward, stopping when she noticed his hair. "That is not Nate!"

Zach drew rein at the corral. "No, it's Scott Kendall, Ma. He took a spill and split his noggin. Pa says he won't last long without your help."

Winona gazed into the pines. "Where is your father?"

Louisa answered. "Last we saw, a grizzly was after him. He was leading it off so it wouldn't attack us. I don't mind telling you, Mrs. King, that he has more sand than most ten men I've known."

Zach, for a reason he couldn't fathom, felt himself grow as hot as a glowing ember in their fireplace. "I'm going to help him as soon we get Mr. Kendall inside."

It took some doing, even with the three of them. Winona had Evelyn strip the quilt off the bed and then deposited the unconscious man on it. She examined his wound, agreeing with her husband's assessment. Unless it was tended quickly their friend would die. "Zach, ride to the lake and fill the water bucket. We'll need a lot. Lou, bring me the towels from the corner cupboard. Evelyn, I need those roots we dug up earlier. And the *unda vich quana* from my medicine bag."

The girls bustled to comply, but Zach frowned. He wanted to go help his father. A "no" was on the tip of his tongue, but he swallowed it and rushed out.

Winona sat on the bed and gently pried Scott Kendall's eyes open. The pupils were dilated, always a bad sign. His pulse was slow, his temperature high. In her mind's eye she flashed back to when she was fourteen, to the time a male cousin received a horrible gash on the temple from a war club in a battle with the Sioux. The healers had done all they could, but her cousin hadn't lasted a week.

Evelyn brought the leather pouch. "How is he?"

"We might lose him," Winona admitted.

"See? This is just what we were talking about, Ma. How can God let bad things happen to a good man like Mr. Kendall?"

Winona put a hand on her daughter's shoulder. "Your father would say that accidents happen. That life isn't perfect. That one of us could step on a rattlesnake tomorrow and die, not because God wanted us to step on it but because we were in the wrong place at the wrong time." She paused. "My people would say that good and bad have both been with us for as long as there have been people. That Coyote, the father of the Shoshones, the Trickster, as we call him, has given us much that is good but also delights in causing much mischief."

"But what do *you* say?"

Winona chose her next words carefully. "Life is a gift, little one. We are born, we live as many winters as we are given, and we die. That is how it is, how it has always been, and how it will always be." Evelyn started to speak, but Winona touched a finger to her lips to shush her. "Let me finish, please. The journey we make from the cradle-board to the grave is not an easy one. There are moments of great joy, as when you were born. There are moments of great sorrow, as when your uncle was killed by the Piegans. There are good things and there are bad things. We don't always plan for them to happen. They just do." Winona pointed at their bookshelf. "In your father's holy book it says that the Great Mystery makes the sun rise on the evil and on the good, and sends rain on the just and the unjust. The sunshine and the rain fall on all our heads, and we must take each as they come. Do you see now?"

"Yes. Thanks." Setting down the medicine bag, Evelyn went to get the roots by the washbasin.

Winona shook her head in amusement. *That was it?* She supposed that she shouldn't be surprised. Children were much more open than adults, much more willing to take a teaching to heart without quibbling over every little detail. Oh, Evelyn would digest what they had talked about and pose more questions later on. But for now the child was satisfied, and Winona should be, too.

Suddenly the bed began to shake. Scott Kendall was convulsing, his back arched, his arms and legs shaking like trees in a chinook. She pressed on his shoulders, but it was like trying to hold down a bucking stallion.

"What's the matter?" Louisa cried, running to help. "What's wrong with him?"

It was readily apparent. Scott Kendall was dying.

Chapter Three

The furious silvertip caught Nate King by surprise. Thinking it was about to give up, Nate was caught off guard when it suddenly renewed its pursuit, charging the bay in a burst of bestial rage. He slapped his legs and lashed the reins, but he was a shade too slow. The bay squealed in agony as claws that could pulverize bone sliced into its flank. And then they were in the clear, racing madly westward with the griz virtually breathing down Nate's neck.

The bear was persistent beyond belief, more so than any Nate had ever come across. It wouldn't relent. For minutes on end the chase continued. Again and again the brute swung but missed.

They shot out of the trees into a meadow, and Nate gave the bay its head. On open ground the horse had an edge. With nerve-racking slowness they began to pull ahead.

Nate looked back on hearing the grizzly roar in frustration. Exerting itself to its limit, the beast was able to maintain the pace for another hundred yards. Finally, though, it exhausted its store of stamina. The thudding paws slowed. The bear uttered several last irate growls as it came to a halt, and if looks could kill, the blazing hatred in its eyes would reduce Nate and the bay to charred cinders.

Nate didn't slow down until he had gone another quarter of a mile. Enough powder was left in the powder horn to reload one of his pistols. He did so while watching to see what the bear would do next. Should it venture deeper into the valley, he would kill it. He'd have no choice. It posed too dire a threat to his family.

For the longest while the griz just stood there, sides heaving, head hung low. When it recovered, it turned to the left—into the valley—and Nate tensed. But it walked only a few dozen feet, raised its head to sniff the air, then pivoted and shambled to the south.

Nate relaxed at last. Wiping his forehead with a sleeve, he headed home. The bay was tired, but Nate held it to a trot out of concern for Scott Kendall. True friends like Kendall were as rare as white buffalo and should be valued all the more because of their rarity. The few Nate had, he would do anything for. And they for him.

Back in the States it was different. There, people tended to take their friends for granted. They got together once or twice a week for ale or rum at the local tavern, or maybe a night on the town. The whole basis for their friendship was to have fun, to amuse themselves at idle diversions. Consequently, their friendships were often as shallow as their pastimes. A man might boast, "Oh, I have a ton of friends!" when in that "ton" there wasn't one who would stand by his side when his life was at risk.

In the wilderness, where day-to-day life was fraught with menace, the quality of a man's friends was of paramount importance. A man had to know they would stick by him, come what may. When blood-crazed Piegans were closing in wasn't the time to find out someone had the backbone of a snail.

In the wilderness friends depended on one another to

an extraordinary degree. They had to. And in doing so they grew closer, becoming more like brothers, forging a bond so strong each would do anything for the other. Nate would rather have a paltry handful of real friends than a "ton" of casual acquaintances masquerading as the real article. Real gold was always preferable to fool's gold.

Smoke was rising from the cabin's chimney when Nate reined up at the corral. The wound the bay had suffered wasn't deep and would keep awhile. He'd get to it as soon as he checked on Kendall. Hurrying around the corner, he saw his son emerge with a bucket in hand. "How's Scott?"

Zach was on his second trip to the lake. "Pa!" he exclaimed, glad to see his father unharmed. "You shook the griz!"

"It took some doing," Nate said.

"Mr. Kendall is in a bad way. He had convulsions a while ago, but Ma got him quieted down. Now she's boiling water and wants more."

"Then off you go."

Nate stepped indoors and was immediately buffeted by a wave of heat. Evelyn was adding a log to the crackling fire. His wife was beside the bed, applying a damp cloth to Scott Kendall's flushed face. "How bad is he?"

"Husband!" Winona was overjoyed, but she didn't rush into his arms as other women would have done. Her expression conveyed the depth of her love as eloquently as any hug. "I have gotten some herbs into him, but if he lasts another day it will be what you whites call a miracle."

From the fireplace rose a shriek of pure delight. "Pa! You're all right!" Evelyn flew at her father and leaped into his arms, squeezing him in glee. "Zach and Lou told us about the bear."

"Where's Louisa?"

Winona looked up. "I sent her after some of the yellow

flowers that help reduce fever. She will not be back for a while yet."

"What can I do?" Nate offered.

"Help me get Scott's buckskins and moccasins off. Then we need to bathe him often to keep his temperature down."

For the next half an hour Nate was so busy he gave little thought to the question uppermost in his mind. Zach returned, filled the sink, and went for a third bucketful, Evelyn tagging along. All that could be done for their friend had been done, and as Nate wrung out the cloth, Winona stretched and gave voice to what puzzled him the most.

"Why did Scott try to come over the south ridge? He knows how treacherous it is. What could he have been thinking?"

"He had to be in a great hurry to reach us, so great he figured the risk worth it" was the only conclusion Nate could come to.

"Which has me worried, husband. There is only one reason he would be so reckless. Scott is not the kind to take needless chances."

No, he isn't, Nate mused, and realized what he had to do. "As soon as Lou gets back, I'm leaving for the Kendall place to check on Lisa and Vail Marie. Will you be all right here while I'm gone?"

Winona gave him a quizzical look. "Need you ask?"

Nate chuckled. Indian women in general, and his wife in particular, never needed coddling. They were as self-reliant as any man and resented being treated as inferior. His wife had made that plain shortly after their marriage began. For the first few weeks he had pampered Winona silly, acting as if she were the Queen of Sheba. Then one evening after supper she had reached across the table, clasped his hands in hers, and bluntly asked, "Why do you treat me like a child, my husband?"

Nate had been so shocked, he'd sat there speechless.

"You insist on going everywhere with me. You won't let me ride alone. You even guard me when I go to the lake. In the cabin you always hover over me, like a sparrow over its young. You are always underfoot, doing things when I have not asked you. If I lick my lips, you bring me a glass of water. If I comment I am hungry, you leap to bring me pemmican. Why do you do all this?"

"I love you," Nate had blurted.

"And I love you. But this is not love. This is smothering. You upset me, husband, by not letting me do things on my own. I am a grown woman. I can take care of myself. And I take great pride in being able to do so. In not being a burden on you. Do you understand?"

At the time Nate hadn't, but he'd mumbled that he did and from then on he'd tried his best not to "smother" her. At length he came to see what she meant, and admired her all the more for being so self-sufficient. It was a source of unending pride that so independent a woman had chosen to give her heart to him because she rated him worthy of her affection.

So now, giving Winona a kiss on the cheek, Nate walked to the cupboard and took down a tin filled with pemmican and another crammed with jerked venison. He filled a parfleche with enough to last a week, then filled his powder horn from the keg of black powder in the far corner.

"What can be keeping Lou?" Winona asked. "It should not take her this long."

"Maybe she had trouble finding the flowers you needed."

"I told her right where they are. It must be something else."

Louisa May Clark had found the hill easily enough, as well as the rocky area beyond where the yellow flowers grew. She dismounted and moved briskly from plant to plant, pulling them out by the roots. Winona had said a dozen would suffice, but Lou decided to pluck an extra eight or nine to be sure. Scrappy little devils, they resisted being uprooted, and she was caked with perspiration before she was half done.

A strident screech drew Lou's gaze overhead, to a hawk soaring high on the air currents. It sailed in wide loops in search of prey, its shadow flitting across the ground as if it were a separate creature. A smaller hawk, the female, winged on high to join her mate.

The pair made Lou think of Zach. Before long they would be just like those hawks, the two of them together forever, doing everything as a couple, always at one another's side until death did them part. She couldn't wait.

Being in love made Lou giddy. She hadn't foreseen how glorious it was, how deliriously grand. Her mother and father had been in love, but in their later years they spent so much time bickering it was a wonder they shared the same roof. Lou's marriage wasn't going to turn out like theirs did. In twenty years Zach and she would still be just as much in love as they were at that very moment. They wouldn't fight, they'd never squabble. They would get along as a married couple should, in perfect harmony.

The ring of a hoof on stone shifted Lou's attention toward the mare. An impatient critter, it didn't much like waiting under a blistering sun for her to finish. "Hold your horses," she said, and giggled. *Telling a horse to hold its horses!* Too bad Zach wasn't there to hear her. He'd have a merry laugh.

Rising, Lou went to the next plant. She hunkered, gripped the bottom of the stem, and prepared to lever upward.

The mare stomped again, nickering.

"You don't listen worth beans, do you?" Lou remarked. It was staring at her in a most peculiar fashion. "Behave or you won't get any oats tonight." The grain was hard to come by, and a rare treat.

Lou firmed her hold and was starting to uncoil when it occurred to her that the mare wasn't staring at her—but *past* her. She glanced over a shoulder and felt her insides churn. Winding down a slope to the west was a line of seven riders, and while they were too far away for her to identify, something in how they rode told her they were Indians.

Lou forgot about gathering more plants. Scooping up those she had already collected, she ran to the mare and stuffed them into a saddlebag. The war party—if that is what it was—had several hundred yards to cover before it reached the hill. She would be well on her way to the cabin to alert the Kings.

Swinging up, Lou reined the sorrel around. She had gone only several yards when she stopped in consternation. Approaching from the southwest were seven more warriors! They had spotted her and were spreading out to cut off her escape!

"Not if I can help it," Lou said grimly. She was not going to let the Kings be taken by surprise. When her father was slain, she'd had to stand by and do nothing; she would be damned if she would fail her new family as she had failed him.

"Heeyaw!" Lou jabbed her heels and fled, heading due east to swing wide of the bunch to the south. But no sooner did she break into a gallop than they did likewise, paralleling her, evidently intent on cutting her off. *They must know where the cabin is!* she deduced, with growing dread. To make matters worse, the warriors to the west had also given chase. Her only other recourse was to head north, but that would take her farther from the Kings.

Lou hunched forward in case the hostiles weren't of a mind to take her alive. They had bows and lances, and the leader had a rifle. She assumed he was the leader, anyway, since he was in front of the rest and she had seen him gesturing at the others as if giving orders.

The mare was game but tired. In the past few hours it had been ridden at breakneck speed from the cabin to the ridge where Kendall had his mishap, then been ridden almost as fast back to the cabin and from there to the hill where the flowers grew. Now, when Lou needed it most, it was flagging.

A warrior to the west whooped and shouted. The tall Indian leading the group to the south responded, and within seconds those to the west were spreading out just as the others had done.

Unbidden, memories of her father's final moments washed over Lou. She recalled all too vividly how his blood had spurted. She remembered how stupefied he had been, remembered the sorrow that etched his features. Until the day she died she would be haunted by the look of love in his eyes as his life faded. That one look had made up for all the days and months and years when he hardly ever told her he cared. She could count the times he had said "I love you, daughter!" on one hand. To be fair, though, her pa had hardly ever said it to her mother, either. *What is it about men that they find it so hard to express their feelings?*

Another shout brought an end to Lou's reverie. A stocky warrior on a pinto had pulled well ahead of the Indians to the south and was angling toward her. He was smiling as if it were a great game, but his smile faded when Lou swiveled and pointed the Hawken at him. The warrior looked at the leader, who nodded and motioned, and the man kept on coming.

Lou thumbed back the hammer. She would die before she would let them take her. If nothing else, the Kings might hear the shot and be forewarned.

"Do you reckon something happened to her, Pa?"

Nate King found his son's anxiety amusing. Louisa's absence could be explained by any number of ordinary events, everything from the mare throwing a shoe to Lou confusing Winona's directions and not being able to find the flowers.

Zach rose in the stirrups to scour the terrain ahead. "I get so worried about her sometimes, it hurts. Do you ever feel that way when Ma is in trouble?"

"Odds are, Lou is just fine, son," Nate stressed. "But yes. I've fretted about your ma something awful on occasion. It can't be helped. Not when you care for someone as much as we care for them."

"I wish Lou had waited for me to get back," Zach complained. "I should have gone with her. She has no business traipsing around alone."

Nate opened his mouth to relate his own dealings with Winona, but changed his mind. Some lessons had to be learned through personal experience. Louisa had a lot of spunk. She would put Zachary in his place eventually, all on her own.

"I never knew it would be like this."

"What would?"

Zach replied in a whisper, "Love."

"It isn't what you expected?"

"Blazes, Pa. Not at all. When I'm around Lou it's like I'm not me, if that makes any sense. My thoughts get all jumbled. It's worse when she touches me. My mind goes as blank as a slate." Zach gnawed on his lower lip. "When we're apart, she's all I think about. I worry every minute. Like now." He stared hard at Nate. "What in tarnation is wrong with me?"

"Nothing. You're as normal as the rest of us."

"Is this what it was like for you? When you met Ma?"

"It's still like that," Nate confessed. "Only, I don't let it affect me as much."

"I don't see how. I always thought that when I met the woman of my dreams, I'd go around as happy as a lark. Now I spend half my time feeling sickly. What do they call that?"

"Love."

Zach blinked, then laughed, and Nate couldn't help but join in. It had been months since they'd had a father-son talk, which bothered Nate some. Until Zach turned twelve, or thereabouts, they'd had talks like this all the time. But once Zachary became a teenager, he no longer seemed to value Nate's opinion on anything.

"Can I ask you another question?" Zach inquired. Normally, he would come right out with it. But this one was so important, he was half afraid of what his father would say.

"I'm always here for you."

"I know." Zach girded himself. "Do you think I'm doing the right thing? By taking Lou as my wife, I mean?"

"I have no say in it, son." Nate wasn't hedging. He truly did feel it wasn't his rightful place to meddle in his son's personal affairs. There came a time when every nestling had to learn to fly under their own power. And in no case was this more true than in the realm ruled by Cupid.

"Please, Pa. I'd really be grateful."

Zach's bearing gave Nate an inkling of how crucial his reply was. What he said next could change the youth's life forever. "Whether I like Lou or not isn't important. It's whether *you* do." Nate saw his son's mouth curl downward. "But I've made no secret of how fond I am of her. She'll be a fine wife and mother." Suddenly Nate spied movement to the northwest. A rider, perhaps? It must be Louisa on her way back. Nate went on. "Are you doing the right thing? If you love her, if she's won your soul, then it's the *only* thing to do. You can't deny fate."

"Do you think we were meant to be together?"

"If a man's meant to drown, he'll drown in the desert," Nate quoted a favorite saying. "If we're meant to meet a certain woman, we'll meet her no matter what we do in our lives." The movement had stopped, but Nate couldn't shake the notion it had been someone on horseback.

"So you're saying that Lou and I were matched up somehow before we were even born? That even if I'd gone off to live with the Shoshones, she and I would have somehow fallen in love?" Zach wasn't a big believer in Fate or Providence, or whatever it was called. His outlook was that things "just happened." Take, for instance, a trapper out working a trapline when a mountain lion jumps him. No one planned for the painter to attack that trapper. It was a random circumstance, a fluke. The same applied to his meeting Louisa.

"Something like that, yes."

"I think—" Zach began, but got no further. To the north a rider galloped into sight, a lithe figure on a small mare, riding pell-mell to the east. "There's Lou!" He was so glad, he showed more teeth than a raccoon that had stumbled on a pond full of frogs. "But where in the world is she going?"

A ragged line of painted warriors provided the answer. The foremost was a hefty warrior on a pinto who would overtake the mare in another fifty or sixty yards.

"Hostiles!" Zach cried, and in a twinkling he was gone, quirting the dun like a madman.

As always, Nate's bay responded to the slightest pressure and he was off after the dun like a hound after a rabbit. But he couldn't catch up. Zach's dun was more than a match for any horse, which had a lot to do with why Nate had traded the Nez Percé for it. To a frontiersman, a reliable mount was worth more than all the precious gems in the world. Nate called for his son to wait, but he might as well ask the moon not to rise.

Zach heard his father, dimly. His blood was roaring in his veins, his whole body was aflame. He choked down frustration and outrage as the stocky warrior reduced the gap. Another minute and the man would have her.

Louisa shared that view. She had held off firing out of fear that killing one of her pursuers would incite the rest to do her in. Now she couldn't wait any longer. Extending the Hawken, she fired at the warrior's stout chest. It should have blown a hole in him the size of a melon. But a fraction of a second before the sizzling lead and spewing smoke belched from the muzzle, the man performed an astounding trick; he dropped onto the far side of his mount, hanging by a crooked elbow and a bent knee. The shot missed, and the warrior, unharmed, rose up onto the pinto's back.

Lou clawed at a pistol. It was sliding clear when a bronzed hand fell on her wrist. Twisting, she was nose to nose with the smirking warrior. She tried to bring the flintlock to bear, but his fingers were an iron vise. Her strength was no match for his. "Let go!" she protested, struggling.

The warrior did another amazing thing. He released his reins and let the pinto run unguided, then lunged for *her* reins to bring her to a stop. "Noooo!" Lou wailed, pushing at his other hand. Leaning closer, the warrior tried again and almost snagged them. She couldn't fend him off for long. So she didn't try.

Sweeping her leg up, Lou kicked him in the ribs. She was praying she could drive him away, but she did even better. He swayed, lost his grip on her wrist, and was on the verge of falling. Instantly, Lou brought up her leg to kick him a second time. But the warrior was resourceful. His hand wrapped around her calf and pulled. Lou futilely clutched the saddle as she was ripped from her perch as if she weighed no more than a feather. Corded arms looped around her waist. She had the sensation of falling and a mild jolt. The warrior had absorbed most of the impact on his shoulder, then rolled.

Lou made another stab for a pistol, but her captor tore it from her belt and started saying the same words over and over. Words that were so much gibberish. For all she knew, he was telling her to behave or he would slit her throat. She scrambled to one side, but a steely grip on her lower leg foiled her escape.

"Let go of me!" Lou railed. She had lost her rifle and one of her pistols, and the second flintlock was pinned underneath her. But the butcher knife strapped to her side was still there. Whipping it out, she resolved to sell her life dearly.

The warrior was grinning, or as Lou believed, *leering*

at her, which fueled her anger. She thrust at his chest, only to have her wrist snared. Again the warrior addressed her, urgently, excitedly. Was it her final warning? Lou punched at his nose, striking his cheek when he jerked aside.

With a powerful heave, the man flung her onto her back and straddled her, pinning her arms and shoulders. Lou bucked upward, but he was too heavy. Bitter tears formed as she sought to throw him off any way she could.

That was when hooves thundered, and Lou figured the other Indians had arrived. But flying toward her was the one person she cherished above all others! "Zach!" she cried.

Zach King was beside himself, boiling like a cauldron, overcome by a burning need to rip, to rend, to slay the warrior who had dared threaten his woman. He snapped up his rifle, but the angle was wrong; he might hit Louisa. Reversing his grip, he held it poised to club and smash.

The weight on Louisa lifted. The Indian had risen and faced Zach, his arms at his sides, making no effort to defend himself. Its significance was lost on her. "You're about to meet your Maker!" she gloated.

A dark hand was raised, but not to employ a weapon. The warrior held it palm out, the universal sign of friendly greeting.

Louisa rose onto her elbows, bewildered. *What was the Indian trying to pull?* He was smiling at Zach even though the Hawken was still upraised to bash his brains out. *It had to be a trick*, she told herself. Then, behind Zach, Nate King appeared, riding as if his life depended on it. Nate was focused on his son, not on the Indian. Lou's intuition flared. Pushing onto her knees, she saw that the rest of the warriors had stopped to observe the outcome. Her name was yelled by Nate, the rest of what he said drowned out by the hammering din. Nate pointed at the stocky warrior, then at her.

Lou could never say what made her do what she did next. A hunch? Instinct? She sprang to her feet and leaped in front of the warrior heartbeats before Zach reached them. Elevating her arms, she screamed, "No! No! I'm not hurt! Don't do it!" But he didn't hear her.

Sunlight bathed the smooth stock of the Hawken as it arced toward her skull.

Chapter Four

Raw, pure emotion is like a tornado. No force on earth can stand against it. Zachary King found that out when he fell hopelessly in love with Louisa May Clark. Until she came along, Zach had prided himself on his self-control. Like the seasoned Shoshone warriors he admired, he'd kept a tight rein on his emotions at all times. Rarely did he let sentiment overrule his judgment.

In the heat of combat a man couldn't let sentiment overwhelm reason. Hatred, anger, unchecked fury, they all made warriors careless, and careless warriors were soon dead ones. Older Shoshones were constantly admonishing younger ones to always stay clam, especially in warfare. As Drags the Rope once said, "He who keeps his head keeps his life."

Zach had liked to think of himself as having a will of steel, as being the master of his own destiny. *Nothing* could ever affect him, because he wouldn't let it. His emotions were under his complete control.

Then Lou walked into his life. His heart—that great betrayer—melted like so much wax, and before he knew it he was like a puppy with a new master. He adored her. Craved her. Couldn't think of living without her. Dwelled on her every minute of every day. Being with her made him float on air. He had never known anything to compare with his feelings for her. He'd never suspected the tremendous power love had over those held in its sway.

Zach had resisted at first. He'd balked at opening his heart fully and tried to tell himself that he wasn't really in love, that there must be another explanation, that the feeling would pass in time. Instead, though, it grew stronger. And as it did, he'd noticed other strange things happening to him. All he had to do was *think* about Louisa being in danger and his blood would race, his mind whirl. It triggered a bewildering reaction deep down inside of him, a reaction he didn't quite understand and could in no way control.

Like now.

The sight of his beloved being threatened filled Zach with boiling rage. Rage so potent, so strong, he lost all conscious control of his being. A ferocious roaring filled his ears. The world around him was shrouded by a haze, except for Lou and the warrior. A reddish haze it was, like a mist made of fine particles of blood. There was a strange constriction in his throat. And he couldn't hear anything. All sounds were drowned out by the roaring.

Zach bore down on the pair in a state of total bloodlust. He did not think about what he was doing, he simply *did* it. He was going to kill the warrior manhandling Lou, and nothing on God's green earth would stop him. To that end, he swept the Hawken overhead to crush the man's skull. In his haze he saw only the warrior's head, only the spot where he was going to strike.

Then another head appeared, the loveliest face ever sculpted by the hand of man or Maker. Zach recognized Lou, but it was as if the part of him that did was separate from the rest of him and had no control over what his body did. For although he knew she had bounded in front of him, he couldn't stop himself from swinging the

Hawken. His roiling rage would not be denied. It controlled him, not the other way around.

As the heavy stock arced toward the upturned face of the girl he cherished, Zach screamed. Not out loud. Deep inside. A cry torn from the depths of his soul. A cry of fear, of desperation, of torment. A cry so piercing, it did what he could not do by willpower alone. It dissolved the red haze in a shattering swell of clamorous sound, and suddenly he was able to think and feel and hear.

With the Hawken less than a foot from its unintended target, Zach wrenched to the right. He couldn't stop the swing, but he could expend its force in midair by throwing himself from the saddle as the rifle descended so that when the stock was at its lowest point, it cleaved air instead of smashing into Lou. He fell off the far side of the dun, which slowed as soon as he was no longer on it. Regaining his feet with the alacrity of a bobcat, Zach sought to level the rifle, but Lou leaped into his arms.

"You're here! For a second there I thought I was a goner!"

The warrior hadn't moved. His hand aloft, he smiled.

Nate King arrived, reining up and declaring in relief, "Thank God! If you'd killed him, son, there would be hell to pay." The other warriors were calmly advancing. None employed their weapons.

Zach finally got a good look at the man he had been about to kill. The warrior's buckskins, the style of his braided hair, the kind of moccasins he wore, all identified him as an Ute. The full import of what Zach had almost done made him wince. For years the Utes had tried to drive his family off, and it was only after his father rendered the tribe a valuable service that they were allowed to go on living in the valley in peace. Had Zach slain that warrior, the Utes would no longer be obligated to hold up their end of the truce. His family would be worse off than ever, because the Utes would be out for revenge this time and wouldn't stop until they got it.

Nate was also keenly aware of how close they had come to reaping disaster. Placing his Hawken across his thighs, he waited until the rest of the Utes had come to a stop. Then, facing the tall leader, he extended the first and second fingers on his right hand, touched them to his lips, and brought them straight out from his mouth. Pausing, he stuck his index finger straight up. It was sign language for "brother."

The leader smiled and responded, his hands flowing smoothly, "My heart happy see you, Grizzly Killer."

Nate was quite fluent in sign, the system of hand symbols used by nearly all the plains tribes and many of those in the mountains. He relied on it in most of his dealings with them. And as was his usual practice, he mentally filled in words sign talk didn't include, such as the common articles "and," "it," and "the"—among others. "I am happy to you see also, Two Owls."

Graying at the temples, the tall Ute had kindly features. Nate had known him for sixteen years, ever since the time they paired up to drive marauding Blackfeet off. Much later, as a result of the friendship they had forged, Two Owls had come to Nate for help in another matter.

In a distant part of the Rockies was a special valley that had the distinction of being one of the few spots where ash trees grew in great number. Both the Utes and the Shoshones preferred ash above all other wood for fashioning bows, so for many winters they had shared the valley, each going there at different times to gather what they needed.

One day, thanks to hotheads on both sides, blood was spilled, which led to an all-out war between the two tribes. Saddened by the loss of lives, Two Owls had come to Nate to arrange a lasting peace. Out of gratitude, Two Owls pledged that for as long as the Kings lived in the mountains, the Utes wouldn't molest them.

Now here was Two Owls once again, as kindly as ever but painted for war and bearing the rifle Nate had given him as a token of the high esteem in which Nate held him. "What brings my friend here?" Nate asked.

The Ute leader was studying Louisa. "Who is this new one? Your daughter could not have grown this big since last we met."

"She is my son's woman," Nate explained.

"She rides well, but she is scrawny. A man should have a woman with big breasts to pillow his head at night."

Nate was glad Lou couldn't understand what they were signing. "Did my brother come all this way to talk about the female body?"

Two Owls sobered. "We hunt killers of my people, Grizzly Killer."

Jumping to conclusions, Nate said, "Are they white men? Have you come to ask my help in tracking them down?"

"They are Indians. But not any my people have ever seen. They come from far to the south, from far beyond where even the Corn Eaters live."

The Corn Eaters? Nate had never heard of them, and plied Two Owls with questions. It turned out they were a poor tribe who dwelled on the banks of a stream the Utes called Corn Creek. A peaceful people who would rather flee than fight, the Corn Eaters were too weak to be considered worthy enemies. So the Utes left them in peace.

"It was the Corn Eaters who warned us of the invaders," Two Owls revealed. "They sent a runner who told us a large war party had attacked them and driven everyone off, then ridden into our land." Two Owls chuckled. "The Corn Eaters are wonderful liars. We found the tracks of these invaders, and there are but twelve."

"Your people clashed with them?"

"The invaders came on a hunting party from my village and killed all seven men. We found the bodies. By then the invaders had moved on, to the northwest, in your direction."

"You tracked them into my valley?"

"No. They are skillful, these savages. We lost their trail four sleeps to the south and have been searching for them since. I was worried they had paid you a visit and came to see if you and your family were well."

"Your friendship makes my heart warm."

"Have you seen any sign of these men, Grizzly Killer?"

"Not so much as a track. The only visitor we have had is a white brother. You know him." Nate said the name aloud. "Scott Kendall."

"The singer. He is a good man. When any of my people stop at his lodge, he always shares food. How is he?"

"He suffered a fall."

"His family is well? His sweet wife and little girl?"

"So far as I know," Nate said, and was jarred to his core by a rush of insight. An awful premonition seized him, a horrible insight into why Scott Kendall had been in such an all-fired hurry, into why Kendall had taken his life into his hands by trying to negotiate that ridge.

Two Owls was not deemed wise for nothing. "What is wrong, my brother?"

"You say that you lost the trail four days south of here?"

"Yes."

That isn't far from the Kendall homestead, Nate reflected. His unease worsened, and he was more eager than ever to reach the Kendall cabin and verify that Lisa and Vail Marie were safe. He signed his concern to Two Owls.

"We believe the strangers have gone farther north. But we will stop at your friend's lodge on our way back to our village."

"I will reach it long before then," Nate signed, then switched to the disaster that had been narrowly averted. "I apologize, for my son, for what just happened. In his fear for his woman his eyes were blinded."

"We are as much to blame as he is," Two Owls replied. "When she saw us, I could tell she was afraid. She was riding very recklessly. I thought she might hurt herself. So I had Otter Tail catch her. His horse is fastest."

The stocky warrior had climbed back onto his pinto and was affectionately patting its neck.

Lou couldn't make hide nor hair of what her future father-in-law and the tall Indian were signing. Recently, Zach had begun to teach her sign, but all she knew were a few basic gestures.

For his part, Zach couldn't take his eyes off the girl of his dreams. The close shave had rekindled the smoldering inferno that forever burned in his breast. He had come so close to losing her! Worse, *he* was the one who had nearly done her in. He yearned to take her into his arms and never let go, but he couldn't so much as touch her with his pa and the Utes there. It would be too embarrassing.

"Would you like to come to my lodge?" Nate asked. "We would be happy to have you."

"Another day," Two Owls responded. "We can cover much ground before the sun goes down. And I must learn whether these strangers mean to cause my people more harm or have left our territory."

"Ride with care," Nate signed.

The Utes did not waste another moment. At a motion by their leader they filed northward, spreading out so they were an arrow's flight apart, heads bent to find sign. In no time the vegetation swallowed them.

"Acquaintances of yours, I gather?" Lou said to Nate. "If I'd known they weren't hostiles, I wouldn't have panicked."

"Better safe than sorry," Nate replied, using the time-worn phrase. "How were you to know? If they'd been Blackfeet or Bloods, we might not have gotten to you in time." He lifted his reins. "I'm heading back. Coming with me, son?"

The question broke Zach's spell. "We'll be along directly, Pa," he answered. He wanted a few minutes alone with Lou.

Nate glanced at her. "Did you collect any of those flowers my wife wanted?"

"Enough, I hope." Lou removed the parfleche from her mare and handed it up to him. "If she needs more, I'll gladly pick them."

Hefting the beaded pouch, Nate said, "This should do. Don't dally too long, you two."

Neither Zach nor Lou spoke until the elder King was lost amid the pines. Then Zach tenderly took her into his arms. "I was so scared I'd lost you." The silken feel of her skin, of her strands of hair entwined with his fingers, the contours of her body against his own, all stirred him as nothing in his entire life ever had.

"For a bit there I thought I'd never see you again, either," Lou said, then boldly kissed him on the neck. His mouth lowered. Time lost all meaning as Lou drifted in a sea of pleasurable sensations, a foretaste of the delights she'd experience once they were man and wife.

Zach had a lump in his throat when he broke for air. "I went crazy when I saw him grappling with you," he acknowledged. "As berserk as a wolverine on a rampage. Nothing like that has ever happened to me before."

"I'm flattered, my handsome prince," Lou said, as much to lighten his mood as to take her mind off his potent kisses.

Zach didn't mention that the thought of losing control like that again scared him silly. No true warrior ever succumbed to mindless rages. What if next time Sioux or Pawnees were involved instead of friendly Utes? In his crazed state he would be easy pickings. His blind fury would cost not only his own life but Lou's also.

"We better cut out for the cabin. Your ma might need our help with Mr. Kendall."

About to turn to the dun, Zach clasped her hand. "Louisa . . . "

"Yes?"

"It's hard for me."

"What is?"

"This love stuff."

"It's hard for both of us."

"You too?"

"What did you expect, silly? How many times do you think I've fallen head over heels for a man?" Laughing, Lou tweaked his earlobe.

"I just hope I don't bring you to any grief."

"Goodness gracious. How could you? You'd never do me harm."

No, Zach wouldn't, not on purpose, but another mistake like the one he had just made could snuff out her wick. "I do care for you. You know that, don't you?" he said.

Lou didn't know what to make of his troubled look. He was acting as if he had done wrong by flying to her rescue. But just because he had gotten a little carried away wasn't cause for him to be miserable. "Of course I do. My heart is yours and your heart is mine. Isn't that what we agreed that night down by the lake?"

"Words can't do justice to how I feel," Zach said. He couldn't find the right ones to make plain how upset he was for failing her when she needed him most.

Lou thought he was saying that his love was so deep, so splendid, mere words couldn't do it justice. "You are so sweet," she said, throwing her arms around him.

They kissed, each happy in the belief the other understood.

As much as Nate would rather race home at a gallop, he stuck to a brisk walk. In part this was because of the hard riding the bay had already done that day. Guilt was also a factor, guilt over the claw marks on its hindquarters, which were bleeding again. With all that had occurred since his return, he hadn't washed and tended them as he should. For a frontiersman, for someone who relied on his horse as much as he did his own two legs, it was an unforgivable oversight.

He drew rein at the front door instead of the corral and was inside in a bound. Winona was wiping Scott's brow. Evelyn was playing with the three Shoshone dolls she owned. Briefly, Nate related the run-in with the Utes while his wife busied herself preparing an herbal tea.

"My guess, husband, is that these strange Indians paid the Kendalls a visit."

"That's what I thought at first," Nate remarked. "But I don't know. For starters, Scott would *never* desert his wife and daughter. So long as they were alive he'd stay by their side. And if they *had* been dead, he would go after the men who did it."

"You must leave as soon as you can," Winona said. They had an obligation to their friends—and to themselves. "Take Zach so he can watch your back."

"Nothing doing. With a marauding war party on the prowl, you'll need him here with you. I'm going alone."

"I can take care of myself."

Resting his hands on her shoulders, Nate whispered in her ear, "Can Evelyn?"

Winona was beaten and knew it. She couldn't keep an eye on their daughter every second. And with Evelyn's knack for getting into mischief, someone responsible had to watch over her. Still, Winona refused to yield. "I'll have Louisa to help me."

"What could she do against a dozen hostiles?"

Not much, Winona conceded, although not aloud. "Let me send Stalking Coyote to fetch Shakespeare."

Nate's mentor, Shakespeare McNair, would be all too glad to accompany him, but it would take a full day to reach McNair's and a full day for the ride back. Nate pointed that out, adding, "I can't delay another hour, let alone two days."

In her head Winona agreed with his logic. In her heart she was apprehensive. Lone mountaineers were more apt to fall prey to mishaps—or roving war parties. But as the whites liked to say, "You have me over a barrel."

In their cupboard was a jar filled with an ointment used by Shoshones to treat open wounds. It cut healing time in half, a feat Nate would never have believed had he not seen it proven time and time again. Grabbing the jar, he stepped outside.

In the States many people regarded Indian treatments as so much mumbo jumbo, as a mix of superstition and nonsense. Nate had been similarly inclined until one day he came down sick with an ungodly high temperature and chills. The sickness lasted for over a week, bringing him to death's door. Winona had tried to get some herbs into him, but he had stubbornly refused, branding it a waste of time. Fortunately, McNair had paid them a visit. His mentor had given Nate a tongue-lashing that would blister a demon's ears, then stood by while Winona spoon-fed the herbs into him. Nate's recovery had been little short of remarkable, and from then on Nate never argued with his wife when it came to healing.

The bay was chomping grass. Nate applied the greasy ointment to the cuts, then let the horse drink from the trough by the corral. When he went in, Winona had just finished trickling a cup of tea down Scott Kendall's throat. "Has he come around yet?"

"No. By morning we will know one way or the other." Winona set the cup on the counter. "I will stay up with him all night, or until his fever breaks."

"Let Zach or Lou spell you some," Nate suggested. "No use wearing yourself out. You need to keep your eyes skinned in case that war party shows up." He gazed deep into her eyes, tormented at having to leave with hostiles in the vicinity. "If I had my druthers I'd stay here where I belong. Say you don't want me to go, and I won't."

"You have it to do. No one with a sense of honor could do any less."

"Damn honor. Damn me for being a fool."

Winona smirked and nodded at Evelyn, who was switching dresses on one of her dolls. "Do not talk like that in front of the children, husband. You set a bad example."

They embraced warmly, kissing on the mouth, something they rarely did unless the lanterns were out and everyone else was sound asleep. Winona groaned ever so softly, then clung to him. Something else rarely done. "Take care, my husband. I love you too much and have lived with you too long to lose you now. Come back to me. Please."

"I'll do it or die trying."

The parting was bittersweet. Winona, Evelyn, Zach, and Louisa were all present. Nate tried not to make a fuss, but when it was his daughter's turn, Evelyn wrapped her tiny arms around his thick neck and wouldn't let go, her button nose buried against his chin. Not once, in all the times he had gone off trapping and on other journeys, had she ever behaved this way—as if she would never see him again.

"What's got you so sulky?"

"Nothing, Pa."

"You're a terrible fibber."

Evelyn raised her head. "I just don't want you to end up like Mr. Kendall."

"I won't."

"How can you be so sure, Pa? I used to think you'd always come back safe because God loves us and watches over us. Now I know he doesn't."

Nate could not have been more stunned if she had started foaming at the mouth like a rabid wolf. "I've heard some silly notions in my time, but that's not worth a shovelful of chipmunk tracks."

"Ma told me."

Winona flinched as if she had been pricked by a lance.

Here she thought Evelyn had understood the point she'd tried to make earlier. Apparently she couldn't have been more wrong.

"What did your mother say?"

"That God makes the sun shine on good people and bad people at the same time. He doesn't favor one over the other."

"So?"

"So if you run into those bad men who hurt Mr. Kendall, God won't make any special effort to help you. He'll just sit up in heaven and watch."

Nate lowered Evelyn to the ground and squatted. "You're mixing berries and wild onions, little one. The weather is for everybody. When the sun shines here, it's also shining on the Shoshones and the Flatheads up north and those Apaches way down near Mexico who once stole your ma. God doesn't give one tribe any more sunshine or rain than the other. He lets them all share alike."

"Oh. That's fair."

"It's different when good people and bad people need God's help. Do you think God is going to lend a hand to someone who goes around killing folks just to be mean?"

Evelyn shook her head.

"Smart girl. God watches over those who live the way God wants us to live."

"Then why didn't he look after Mr. Kendall? Mr. Kendall believes in the Almighty."

Nate's grandfather once commented that the hardest questions to answer were those posed by children. Stumped, Nate answered as honestly as he knew how. "That's where we come in. God brought Mr. Kendall to us so we can help him. And his family. That's why I have to go." He kissed her, then mounted. Everyone else was as somber as a thundercloud as he rode out. Twisting, Nate grinned and waved.

"Don't fret none, Pa!" Evelyn hollered. "God will watch over you while you're gone!"

Nate sorely hoped so. But as he passed the corral he loosened the twin pistols under his belt and adjusted his knife sheath so the hilt was within easy reach.

Chapter Five

From far out on the prairie the Rocky Mountains reared like jagged ramparts. Anyone fresh from the States could be forgiven for imagining they resembled a gigantic castle, the high stony walls stretching for as far as the eye could see to the north and south. Drawing closer, awestruck travelers were always dazzled by their imposing height and amazed that even in the hottest summer months snow crowned many of the majestic peaks.

It wasn't until mesmerized pilgrims neared the emerald-green foothills that they would realize the Rockies weren't a solid sawtooth citadel, that the many high summits were broken by scattered valleys and canyons and gorges.

In the upland regions were many lush grassy areas, called "parks" by the mountaineers. It was in one such valley that Nate King had his cabin. Two valleys to the south lay the Kendall homestead. Between them was another "park," and there another couple dwelled.

The three families were the only settlers in that whole region except for Shakespeare McNair, and he wasn't so much a settler as a living part of the mountains themselves. He had lived in the Rockies longer than any living white man, since shortly after the epic journey made by Lewis and Clark.

Nate didn't quite qualify as a "settler" either. He had been a free trapper for years, and as many trappers were wont to do, he had adopted many Indian ways, even going as far as to take a lovely Indian woman as his mate. Or, rather, Winona had taken him, for when he thought about their courtship, he realized she had taken the initiative. He marveled that Winona had endured his awkward, bumbling attempts at romance without complaint, and that she later had been willing to become his wife.

The couple who lived in the next park fit the definition of settlers perfectly. They were easterners who had been enticed into venturing to the frontier, and once there had fallen so in love with nature's beauty, becoming so enamored of the magnificent splendor the Rockies offered, that they had built a cabin and set down roots.

Simon and Felicity Ward were from Boston. They had an accent that tickled Nate's fancy, and were as kind and decent as the year was long. Nate had imitated Shakespeare McNair and become Simon Ward's mentor, passing on the knowledge McNair imparted to him.

Nate had taught Simon how to hunt, how to track. How to tell the age of a print by the texture of the dirt and other factors. How to tell whether a deer was a buck or a doe by the way it urinated. How to judge whether an animal had been walking or running by the length of its stride and the depth of the impressions, Nate was a bottomless well of knowledge, and Simon soaked it up like a sponge.

It delighted Nate no end that Simon had taken to the wilderness like a duck to water. The younger man couldn't get enough of it. He still wore homespun clothes instead of buckskins, and he still thought more like an easterner than a true son of the wilds, but by and large Simon was learning to adapt remarkably fast and Nate had high hopes the Wards would be able to make a go of it.

The Kendalls had been helping out in that regard. Scott had lived in the mountains longer than Simon and was enormously skilled in his own right. He, too, was teaching Simon essential crafts needed to survive.

But their lives were not all work, work, work. At least once a month the three families got together for a day of socializing. The kids frolicked, the women talked about how pigheaded their men were, and the men drank and ate and played cards.

Felicity Ward looked forward to those get-togethers with sharp anticipation. The next one wasn't due to be held for another couple of weeks, but she was on the lookout for visitors just the same. Ever since Scott Kendall had ridden urgently by without a word of explanation, she had been waiting for him to return. Or for someone else to appear.

Felicity had told her husband about Scott's strange behavior. Simon wanted to ride to the Kings and find out what was going on, but Felicity cautioned him to wait a bit. If something was really wrong at the Kendalls', they would find out soon enough and could decide then how best to help.

On this bright, sunny morning Felicity was hanging just-washed clothes on a line stretched from a corner of their cabin to a tree by the stream. Her mouth crammed with clothes pegs, she stretched out a dress and hung it on the rope.

Her husband was off in the woods, checking snares he had set the evening before. Yet another crafty trick taught them by Nate King. "Why waste hours traipsing over hill and dale, wearing yourself to a frazzle hunting," the big mountain man had quipped, "when a snare can do all the work for you? One of Zach's chores when he was growing up was to rig snares at new spots once a week and check them every day. He did a fine job, too. Hardly a night went by that we didn't have something for the supper pot."

Felicity had been sad at the thought of killing sweet little bunnies. But her sadness lasted only as long as her belly was full. Once her stomach took to growling, she thought of them less as sweet little bunnies and more as delicious, nourishing meat. It was amazing how the threat of starvation changed a person's outlook.

Felicity gazed toward the forest, expecting Simon at any time. She hung a shirt and a towel, dropped the last few pegs in the pail she carried them in, and started to turn toward the cabin. Idly, she glanced to the north—and her heart skipped a beat.

Even at that distance there was no mistaking the rider who approached. His size alone betrayed him. As did that big black bay of his, so much larger than most horses, adding to the impression of the rider being a giant among men.

Felicity ran into the cabin to deposit the pail, then gave her hair a quick brushing and smoothed her dress. Silly, really, but she always liked to look her best when company called. Her mother's influence was to blame, for in prim and proper Boston it was unpardonable for a hostess to appear at less than her best. Her mother had been a firm believer in "appearances are everything."

Felicity ran back out. She hoped Simon would return soon. It didn't bode well that Scott Kendall wasn't with their visitor.

Struck by a thought, Felicity dashed back inside, snatched a glass from the cupboard, and raced to the stream to fill it. She had it ready, filled to the brim, when the man she was fond of second only to her husband reined up and gave her one of his charming smiles.

"Howdy, Felicity. It does these tired eyes a world of good to see a sprightly damsel like yourself on such a cheery morning."

"Is it really so cheery?" she responded.

Nate King never ceased to be amazed by feminine intuition. Women had an unnatural ability to divine things they had no rational basis to know. Take Winona. She could sense his feelings, his thoughts, even when he didn't necessarily want her to. She also had a remarkable facility for sensing when others were going to pay them a call. On more than one occasion she had piped up with, "Someone is coming. I can feel it." And sure enough, before too long someone would show up at their place.

Now Nate stiffly dismounted and stretched. He had ridden half the night, stopping only for the bay's benefit, and then only as long as was absolutely necessary. "Where's that husband of yours?"

"Checking snares," Felicity said, giving him the glass. "I saw Scott Kendall go by late the day before yesterday. He was in a pitiable state, and wouldn't hardly speak. Have you seen him? Is he all right?"

Nate was emptying the glass. As he lowered it, a figure ambled from the trees, spotted them, and broke into a run. "Here comes your lesser half now." Grinning, Nate removed his beaver hat and slapped it against his leg to shake out the dust. "How about if I tell both of you all about it over a bowl of soup? Or some of those tasty sweet rolls of yours? I can't stay long, sad to say."

"I'll have some rolls ready in two shakes of a lamb's tail."

Simon Ward arrived as his wife bustled indoors. A young, exuberant man, he tossed the rabbit he carried next to the cabin, then fondly clasped the mountain man's broad shoulders. "Nate! To what do we owe this honor? I've been tempted to ride up and see you, but my wife thought it best I stick around."

"You're lucky she did."

"I am?"

Nate ushered the younger man into the cabin. The couple listened intently as, between bites of Felicity's delicious rolls, he detailed Scott Kendall's accident and Nate's run-in with Two Owls. Nate didn't mince words. They had a right to know exactly how much danger they were in. "From now until we know the war party is shed of our neck of the country, you can't take chances. Never go anywhere unarmed. Never stray far from the cabin unless you're together. Always tether your stock close by at night so you can hear if they raise a racket."

Simon bobbed his chin. "Don't worry. I haven't forgotten what you've taught me. I'll take every precaution."

Felicity was more worried about their friends. "Do you think Lisa and Vail Marie have come to any harm?"

"I'll know tomorrow when I reach their place." Nate wiped his mouth with the back of his sleeve. "Sorry to eat and light a shuck, but I only stopped long enough to fill you in and give my horse a breather." He rose and claimed his Hawken.

Simon and Felicity trailed him, arm in arm. "Do you have any inkling who these intruders are?"

"Not yet," Nate admitted. "Even the Utes are stumped. But we have to keep in mind that whole sections of the West haven't been explored yet. There are parts no white man has ever set foot in. Areas the tribes we do know about shun as bad medicine."

Felicity stared wistfully eastward. His comments reminded her of how isolated they were. It was close to a thousand miles to St. Louis, the nearest city of any consequence. To the west it was another thousand miles to California. Here they were, literally in the middle of nowhere, smack in the center of North America, as alone as if they were on another planet, outsiders in a world not of their making, infants daring to eke out a living in the cruel cradle of the wilderness. At moments like these Felicity regretted leaving Boston, regretted leaving their relatives, abandoning everyone and everything that had been special to her.

Sometimes Felicity wondered what they were trying to prove. Why put their lives in peril for the sake of a dream? Then she would stand on the doorstep and admire the virgin valley, the regal peaks. She would see deer and buffalo grazing, see ravens winging by or maybe a bald eagle high, high in the sky, and her soul would be stirred to its very depths. She would know, in those instants, why she had let Simon talk her into the trek. Why she stayed, and might never return.

It could be summed up in one word, a word more precious than all the others in the English language, a word embodying an ideal over which armies had clashed, an ideal for which men and women down through the ages had been willing to throw their lives away. That word? Freedom.

In the mountains a person was truly free. Wonderfully, gloriously free. To live as they pleased, in any manner they desired. No one told them what to do or how to go about doing it. Politicians and lawyers weren't trying to imprison them behind bars made of ironclad laws. Busybodies weren't snooping into their affairs.

Felicity had never truly understood what real freedom was until she came to the mountains. Which was ironic. Back in Boston she'd always assumed she was as free as any human being on earth, that having society dictate how she conducted her life was part and parcel of freedom itself. The Rockies taught her differently.

Society was a gilded cage. It made living easier in that it provided food, clothing, and shelter. But at a horrendous cost. Since people were no longer able to hunt for their own food, they had to take whatever food was available at the market or butcher's. Since they didn't make their own clothes, they had to wear whatever fashions society decreed was acceptable. And because no one was allowed to plant stakes wherever they wanted, they had to make do with such housing as was available.

Freedom was traded for convenience. Comfort became the be-all and end-all of existence. In exchange for full bellies and warm clothes and soft beds, people were willing to give up the most priceless treasure in all existence.

Felicity thought that inexpressibly sad.

Suddenly a comment by Nate King brought Felicity's musing to an end.

"To be a little safer, you two should cut all the grass around your cabin for forty or fifty feet. And keep it cropped. At night cover the windows with a blanket so no one can shoot you from out in the dark."

The two men shook. "We'll do as you suggest," Simon said. "Don't lose that long hair of yours to those heathens."

The statement gave Nate pause. His friend was basically a good man at heart, but afflicted with a sentiment common among whites—namely, that the majority of Indians were sinful pagans and thus inferior. Knowing Winona had changed Simon's thinking some, but not enough. "They probably think *we're* the heathens, friend," he bantered as he stepped into the stirrups.

Simon chortled. "But we know better, don't we?"

Nate pursed his lips. "Most things that people do are judged right or wrong depending on the time and the place and the folks doing the judging." Touching his hat to Felicity, he slapped his heels against the bay. It was only about ten A.M. With hard riding he could reach the Kendall place by midnight. Hard, hard riding. He regretted having to push the bay, but lives were at stake.

As he traveled, Nate was alert for sign. He saw plenty of evidence of game, but no horse tracks other than those Scott Kendall had made riding north. Paralleling them, Nate discovered that Kendall hadn't stuck to the beaten path. Scott had made a beeline cross-country, riding as recklessly as he had on the ridge. It was amazing a mishap hadn't happened long before then.

With so much ground to cover, Nate had a lot of time to think. He tried not to dwell on his family, home all alone, but he couldn't help it. They were his life, his reason for drawing breath. Should anything happen to them, he would be devastated; he wouldn't care to go on living. He tossed his head to clear it of horrid images of Winona being assaulted. He couldn't stand to even consider the possibility. She was as much a part of him as his internal organs—and infinitely more important.

Funny thing about marriage. Wedlock took two independent people and molded them into one whole. It drew them out of their shells, made them reach out for the other, helped them learn whole new facets to being alive.

Take Winona and him. When they first met he had cared for her in a different way than he did now. Oh, he had loved her, but the love had a different texture than his mature love did—sort of like the difference between coarse burlap and fine silk.

When couples were young, much of their love had to do with how attracted they were to each other physically. Sexually. As they grew older, they became more attracted to the other's personality, to what it was that made that person who they were. Nate's affection for Winona had deepened to the point where he thought of her and him as two halves of the same coin. They were joined at the soul, as it were.

And Nate wouldn't have it any other way. There was a lot about life he didn't understand. Much that puzzled him. But one fact he knew beyond a shadow of uncertainty. Loving another person was the greatest experience anyone could have. Which was why he was so happy for his son.

Louisa genuinely cared for Zach. They were young, but Nate had known Shoshones and others who married even younger. If they would nurture their affection like a farmer nurtured seeds, the bliss they'd share would be beyond belief.

These ramblings, and others, occupied the big trapper for the rest of the day and long into the night. He left the Wards' valley behind and climbed a series of rolling hills into the range that bordered the Kendalls'. From seven miles above sea level he gazed out over the benighted landscape, out over an inky canopy broken by rocky islands.

Sunset had brought the predators from their dens. Bears and painters, wolves and coyotes, bobcats and others roamed in search of prey. Roars, howls, yips, and screeches punctuated the night, along with the screams of creatures that were slain. The bestial chorus might scare greenhorns, but to Nate it was music as sweet as any ever composed by Europe's masters. Countless nights he had drifted asleep serenaded by the feral song.

Nate had to be extra careful, though, and he rode with the Hawken at the ready. Wolves and coyotes posed no threat, but mountain lions and grizzlies were as common as fleas on an old hound dog, and had worse bites. Once, something heavy crashed through brush on his left. Nate brought up the rifle, but whatever it was meandered elsewhere. Another time a painter screeched, so close at hand that the bay nickered and shied.

Even though Nate was accustomed to riding at night, every now and then the murky darkness and the eerie rustling and stirrings got to him, fanning his imagination so that he thought he saw menacing hulks where there were none and heard sinister snarls when it was only the wind.

Nate consoled himself with the thought that even the Shoshones, who had dwelled in the mountains since time out of mind, were prone to making groundless fears out of whole cloth. How else to account for some of the bizarre tales they told? Of red-headed giants that could rip a man's head from his body? Of enormous snakes that lived deep in the bowels of the earth? Of water monsters that upended canoes and ate those who fell out? Most fascinating of all were stories told by the elders of the tribes, accounts of mysterious "little people" who lived deep in the mountains. As savage as sidewinders, the little men attacked every human they caught in their domain, slaying them with tiny arrows shot from tiny bows.

Nate branded the outrageous accounts as ridiculous. But it bothered him that some of the most respected oldsters in the Shoshone nation, men and women he'd met and who seemed as sane as he was, firmly believed the little people existed. A warrior called Two Knives had offered to take him to where the little people could be found, but one thing or another had kept Nate from taking Two Knives up on the kind offer. Maybe one day soon Nate would. He'd take Zach along, perhaps Lou, too, and use it as an excuse to become better acquainted with her. What harm could it do? There wasn't any danger. The little people were a figment of Shoshone imagination, concocted long ago around campfires by ancestors afraid to leave the safety of the firelight for the ominous gloom beyond.

Along toward midnight Nate descended to a spine above the valley the Kendalls called home. Their cabin was situated in a stand of aspens in the middle, beside a spring. Scott had picked wisely. His family had ample water and forage, the trees sheltering them from summer sun and wintry winds.

Nate drew rein to listen. A deathly silence blanketed the valley, unnaturally so since all around the wilderness was alive with sounds and furtive movement. No lantern light shone amid the trees, which was to be expected since the Kendalls normally turned in early, by ten at the very latest.

At a walk, Nate continued. The dull clomp of the bay's hooves seemed louder than they actually were. He had the feeling unseen eyes were upon him but shrugged it off. His nerves were acting up, was all.

High grass swayed in the stiff breeze, like waves on the ocean. Nate held the Hawken at chest height, his spine rigid, fully alert. When a long, sinuous shape parted the blades on his right, he swung around and fixed a hasty bead. But the snaked recoiled and glided elsewhere.

The aspens' leaves shimmered like so many bees' wings, glistening palely in the starlight. Nate was sorry the moon wasn't out. The extra light would help. He stopped again to probe the stand, distinguishing the black outline of the cabin deep in among the slender boles.

Nothing stirred, not even in the horse pen that flanked the rear of the structure. And as Nate recalled, Scott Kendall had a mule that brayed at the slightest of alien sounds.

At close quarters pistols were better than a rifle. Slinging the Hawken, Nate palmed a flintlock, thumbing back the hammer on the .55-caliber smoothbore. A nudge of his knees sent the bay forward. It shared his wariness and advanced slowly, ears erect, nostrils flaring.

The cabin might as well have been a mausoleum for all the signs of life. Nate reined up twenty feet out, slid quietly down, and cat-footed to the corral. As he'd suspected, all the animals were gone. Four horses and the mule.

His back to the wall, Nate edged toward the front corner. A dry leaf crunched underfoot and he froze, awaiting an outcry or a shot. When neither materialized, he moved on. A peek showed no one was in front. Nate sidled to the window. A burlap cover was drawn over it, preventing him from peering within. Ducking, he slid past, unfurled, and sidestepped to the jamb.

The door was open. Not a crack, as it would be to let in fresh air, but standing wide enough for him to enter. It verified the Kendalls weren't home. Lisa would never be so careless.

Nate scanned the interior. Immediately, to forestall being shot, he jerked back. Once again no shots rang out. Sucking in a deep breath, Nate drew his other pistol, then sprang inside, to the right of the doorway. He had a jumbled impression of objects being where they shouldn't, of a table that was supposed to be on the left now in the middle of the room, and of a chest of drawers that had been moved.

Waiting a full minute to confirm he was alone before he moved, Nate straightened and walked to the west window. As he recollected, the Kendalls kept a lantern on a peg close by. It wasn't there.

Nate gingerly felt his way to the fireplace. The wood had long since gone cold. Fishing his fire steel and flint from his possibles bag, he lit a small fire that soon blazed high. After adding more logs from the bin, he rose and turned.

His first impression had been all wrong. The furniture hadn't been moved around. It had been *thrown* every which way. The place was a shambles, everything overturned or upended, torn clothes and broken articles lying willy-nilly. Silverware relatives had sent clear from Massachusetts, tools Scott had used in constructing the cabin, a small crib for Vail Marie's doll, everything and anything had been scattered or shattered or both.

Nate was heartbroken. He had hoped against hope that this wasn't what he would find. He'd prayed the woman and the girl were all right, that when he got there they would greet him as they always did, that there was some other reason for Scott's mad ride other than the marauding war party. Now those hopes were smashed to bits.

Nate moved to the tiny crib. Someone had stomped it to pieces and ripped off the bright cloth Lisa had trimmed it with. Scouring the room for clues to the fate of mother and daughter, Nate noticed the bedroom door ajar. Scott had insisted on a separate room for the adults so they would have some privacy. Vail Marie slept in a recessed nook just past the fireplace.

Fearing what lay beyond, Nate leveled a pistol and crept toward it. A skittering sound brought him up short. A shadow appeared, low down to the floor, and he trained the flintlock on it. He was a hair's width from squeezing the trigger when the source of the shadow shuffled into the light, its small black nose and whiskers twitching.

"What the dickens are you doing in here?" Nate demanded.

The raccoon chittered as if irate at the intrusion, then as nonchalantly as could be waltzed out into the night.

Chuckling, Nate pushed open the bedroom door. His mirth was short-lived. A whirlwind had struck, ripping and shredding and smashing every item. Knives had reduced the bedding to ribbons. An artist's rendering of

Lisa's parents had been hacked apart. Elk antlers Scott had hung above the headboard had been torn off.

The only encouraging sign was that so far Nate had not seen any trace of blood. He backed out, and stiffened.

The bay had whinnied.

Nate ran to the front door, seeking the cause. Crashing tree limbs, crackling brush, and a wild cry spun him to the left just as a huge form erupted from the vegetation almost on top of him. Before he could snap off a shot, a man sprang from a horse straight at him.

Chapter Six

Nate King's reflexes had been honed to the sharpness of a sword's edge by his years in the wilderness. Life in the wild was like a whetstone, sharpening instincts, toning muscles, steeling sinews. The demands of day-to-day living required that those who wanted to survive *must* adapt. Those who didn't never lived long.

Nate had come to think of it as "survival of the quickest." It wasn't how strong a person or an animal was that mattered, or how intelligent, or how high they could fly or how far they could bound in a single leap. In life-and-death situations, at moments when life was in peril, what counted most was how *quick* they were.

Once, several greenhorns visited the King cabin. During the course of a friendly jawing session the subject of staying alive came up. Nate mentioned his belief that quickness was essential, and they had pressed him with questions. A lanky fellow from Ohio wanted to know the difference between being *quick* and being *fast*. Nate responded that quickness had more to do with speed, while being fast merely meant that a person was fleet of foot.

The pilgrim still hadn't understood. So Nate produced a coin and put it in the palm of his hand. He'd told the man to snatch it from him, which the man tried doing several times and couldn't. "You're not very quick," Nate tactfully commented.

"What a silly test. No one could do that. I'd like to see you try." The greenhorn had asked for the coin and held it in his own palm. "Any time you're ready," he'd said with a smirk.

The coin was in Nate's hand before the man finished speaking. The three men had been greatly impressed, but to Nate it was a child's game, a parlor trick. Out in the wild a man had to be that quick, and quicker.

As the figure on the horse flew at him, Nate demonstrated how superbly quick he really was. He leaped backward, into the cabin, before the figure could reach him. The Hawken was level and cocked, his trigger finger curled around the trigger, when the unkempt, wild-eyed rider burst in after him.

Nate had the man dead to rights and could have blown a hole in him the size of a melon. But he didn't fire. Instead he gawked in amazement, blurting out, "Scott? Is that really you?"

Scott Kendall was disheveled, his torn buckskin shirt hanging out, his ripped pants still caked with dirt and grime from his tumble into the talus. The nasty gash on his head wasn't bleeding, but fresh small cuts on his face and neck were. His eyes were saucers, dilated and darting back and forth, his mouth twitching uncontrollably. In his brawny hands was his rifle, which he swung from side to side as if seeking enemies to slay. "Where are they?" he roared. "Lisa! Vail Marie!"

"Scott—" Nate said, letting the Hawken's muzzle dip.

The other mountain man seemed not to hear. Brushing past Nate as if he weren't there, Scott ran about the room like a soul possessed, throwing furniture, looking into cabinets and cupboards, all the while raving, "Where are you? Where are you? Where are you?" Suddenly he ran into the bedroom. There was more crashing and wailing, then he emerged, more haggard than ever. Legs wobbly, he stumbled as if drunk and mewed like a lost kitten, "They're gone! Oh God, they're still gone!"

"Scott?" Nate said again.

Kendall blinked, the wildness fading from his gaze. "Nate? Is that you? What are you doing—" Scott pressed a hand to his brow. "Oh. Now I remember."

Picking up an overturned chair, Nate placed it beside his friend. "Here. Take a seat. I'll fetch you some water from the spring."

"No. I don't need any. I'm fine. Truly fine." Scott eased down, his appearance belying the claim. His features were chalky white, and he poured sweat. His forearms trembled so badly, he had to grip his legs to steady them. Tears filled his eyes as he surveyed the wreckage. "I was hoping they'd returned. That somehow they'd gotten away and made it here on their own. We have to go after them! Now! Before it's too late."

"First things first," Nate responded, taking Kendall's rifle and leaning it against the wall. "How did you recover so soon? And why in the world did Winona let you come after me?"

Scott averted his face. "She didn't, exactly." He licked his lips. "A couple of hours after you'd left, I came to. Winona told me you were on your way here. I begged her to let me go after you, but she wouldn't. She claimed I was too weak."

"You should have listened to her."

"Easy for you to say. We both know what you would've done if it was your wife and child." Scott looked up, and Nate saw a tear trickling down his cheek. "I bided my time until Winona and Zach and everyone had turned in. Then I grabbed my clothes and my possibles and snuck out. My sorrel was plumb worn to a frazzle, so I borrowed that buckskin of yours, the one you usually use as a pack animal." He grew sheepish. "Hope you won't hold it against me. It's not as if I meant to steal it."

"You should have stayed in bed," Nate reiterated. What had been done couldn't be undone. Now the question was: What to do next? "How are you feeling? God's honest truth, mind you."

Scott ran a hand through his tousled hair. "A mite puny, I'm ashamed to admit. Tired. Hungry enough to eat a whole buffalo. And there's a blacksmith in my noggin, pounding on an anvil." A lopsided grin curled his mouth. "Other than that, this coon is fit as a fiddle. We can head out right this minute."

"Like hell." Nate had already come to a decision. "We'll rest up here until first light. You're to get some sleep. If you don't, we're not going anywhere."

"But—" Scott began, and realized it would be useless to argue. "I suppose a few hours' sleep can't hurt. But we light out at dawn, and we don't slack off until my wife and daughter are in my arms again."

Nate gestured. "Were you here when this happened? Did you see who took them?"

"No." Scott said it softly, in abject torment. "I was off hunting. We were low on fresh meat, so I went after a buck."

"You can't blame yourself."

"The hell I can't! If I'd been here, I could've prevented this!"

"If you'd been here, Scott, you would be dead. Didn't Winona tell you what Two Owls said?"

"Yes. She did. That's what fired me up to get here as soon as I could." Despondent, Kendall propped his elbows on his knees and his chin in his hand. "Oh Lord, Nate. What am I to do? Lisa and Vail Marie mean everything to me."

"We'll find them."

Tears were flowing freely. "I can't let myself think

anything else or I'll go crazy in the head. The whole ride up to your place, I was so worried, I couldn't think straight. I didn't stop to rest or eat or anything."

Nate remarked how puzzled he was that his friend hadn't gone after the war party by his lonesome.

Scott's torment worsened. "I started to. When I came back and found the cabin like this, I was beside myself. I followed their tracks to the southwest, all stoked to rub out every last one of those scum. But I lost the trail."

"You?"

"Me." Scott's wide shoulders slumped. "I don't know how they did it, hos, but those devils skunked me proper. It was as if they'd vanished off the face of the earth. I knew that I needed someone even better at reading sign than I am, so I went after you."

Nate was perplexed. First the Utes, then his friend. All were highly competent trackers. Yet the invaders had hoodwinked them as slick as bear grease. The only Indians capable of such a feat were Apaches, but Apaches never roved so far north. "I'll do what I can," he pledged.

Scott gripped Nate's wrist. "You're my last hope. If you fail, my wife and daughter are as good as dead."

Not quite, Nate thought. It was unlikely the war party would slay Lisa and Vail Marie. Kendall had to know that, too, but he was refusing to acknowledge it. Which was for the best. Down that nightmarish road lay rampant rage and the borderland to madness. "Let's try to get some sleep."

"Are you serious? I'm so worried, I won't be able to get a lick of rest until my family is safe."

"Try," Nate said. "As a favor for me."

Scott's spirit wasn't willing, but exhaustion wouldn't be denied. Hardly had they spread out what little bedding could be salvaged and lain down than he was sawing logs loud enough to be heard back in Boston.

Nate stared at the shattered doll's crib, overcome by sympathy. The one aspect of wilderness life he liked least was the ever-present threat to his loved ones. He never knew from one day to the next if his family would still be alive to greet the next dawn. They'd all learned to live with it, to accept the danger as part of their normal routine. Yet it gnawed at him, like a beaver gnawing into wood.

Whenever he left home for any length of time, Nate constantly fretted. Oh, he could shove his worries into a corner of his mind and keep them there if he erected a mental wall. But all it took was the sight of a painter or sign left by an enemy tribe to bring the wall crashing down, and his worry would rush out of that corner like a riled griz out of a den, slashing and chewing at his innards.

Nate drifted off but slept lightly. He long since trained himself to wake up at the slightest noise, an essential skill for any trapper. He'd also learned how to will himself to get up at certain times. If he wanted to be on the go by, say, five in the morning, almost always he would wake up right on the button.

This morning was no exception. Nate had been awake for half an hour and had coffee brewing before Scott Kendall stirred. Dawn wasn't far off when his friend sluggishly sat up and groaned.

"Land sakes. I feel like I've been stomped by a mule. Every part of me that can hurt, does."

"As soon as we have some breakfast, we'll head out."

Scott threw off his blanket. "I couldn't eat if I tried. Let's just mount up and go. Every minute we waste is like a knife in my vitals."

Nate opened his parfleche. Removing the bundle of pemmican, he unwrapped it and held out a piece. "If you want my help, then you do as I say from here on out. We'll do this right or we won't do it at all."

"That's awful harsh, isn't it, pard?" Scott sounded hurt.

Nate didn't think so, not when their lives and those of Lisa and Vail Marie were at stake. So he didn't hold back. "You're not thinking straight. You said so yourself, last night. I don't blame you, because if I were in your moccasins I'd feel the same. But it's made you careless. You almost died. That cracked skull of yours should be all the proof you need that I'm right."

"Sure, I—"

Holding up a hand, Nate cut him off. "One of us has to stay as sharp as a briar, Scott. I'll gladly help track your family down, on the condition that I'm in charge. Do you agree to abide by whatever I say? At all times?" he emphasized, then waited for his friend's reaction. Truth was, Nate would help even if Scott didn't accept, but it would be best for everyone if they came to an understanding before they lit out.

Scott Kendall wrestled with his pride. Part of him balked at what he felt was an unfair demand. Another part realized Nate was imposing on him in his own best interests. He imagined Lisa's lovely face shimmering in the air, and his pride withered. "I reckon this coon has no choice."

"Good." Nate grinned. "My first order as booshway is for you to get some food and coffee into you. Whether you want to or not. You'll need all your strength for what's ahead."

Scott begrudgingly accepted the pemmican and bit off a sizable chunk. "You know," he said, his mouth crammed full, "you're the only person alive I'd let get away with this. I never did like being told what to do."

"Me, neither," Nate said. "And look at what we went and did."

"Huh?"

"We got married."

Scott laughed for the first time since the raid on his cabin. "True enough, hos. The minute we say 'I do,' we're done for. From then on it's 'Honey, do this,' and 'Honey, do that.' Makes a fella wonder if he's got a mind of his own."

Nate agreed, glad his ruse had worked. If there was

one topic that could get a married man to joke and relax, it was wives. Every husband had a hundred stories to tell, usually exaggerated and embellished to the point they'd qualify as epic literature. And the womenfolk were no different. He'd overheard a few of Winona's chats with other ladies and learned they liked poking fun at their husbands just as much as their husbands like poking fun at them.

In this instance, though, the effect didn't last as long as Nate hoped.

"That Lisa!" Scott declared. "I ever tell you about her cleaning ritual? Twice a year we give this place a going-over from top to bottom. She has me move everything outside so she can clean both rooms at once. Well, one spring there were some clouds to the west and I warned her it might rain before she was done. But she thought I was making an excuse to get out of work and had me move all the furniture out anyway."

"Did it rain?"

"Rain? Tarnation! It poured! A regular gully-washer. So there I was, heaving chairs and whatnot in through the door just as fast as I—" Scott stopped, his gaze on the broken table. When he went on, he spoke quietly, almost tenderly. "And what did she do while I was grumbling and fussing and getting soaked to the skin? She laughed, is what she did. She laughed, and when I was all done, she kissed me and—" He could go no further.

Nate filled a battered tin cup. "Gulp a few of these and we'll be on our way."

As Scott accepted it, his features became as flinty as quartz. "I swear by all that's holy, Nate, if they've harmed her or my daughter I'll make them pay. I'll wipe out the whole damn tribe. Just see if I don't."

Nate said nothing. It wasn't his friend talking, it was spite. Usually Scott was the most amiable man alive, always even-tempered, always tolerant of others. Scott wasn't one of those whites who despised Indians simply because they weren't white. He didn't look down his nose at them, as Simon Ward was prone to do. All that might change if the worst came to pass.

Nate was determined to see that it didn't.

The tracks were easy enough to read, at first.

Ten warriors on unshod mounts had approached the cabin from the southwest, dismounted, and taken Lisa by surprise. Afterward, they'd made her and Vail Marie climb on one of the horses in the corral. Leading the rest, the war party had galloped off the same way they had come.

For over two miles the prints were as plain as day. They led up out of the valley and toward a rocky spine. As Nate passed through a verdant track of woodland, he noticed the stump of a low limb recently broken off. Recent, because the exposed wood was still a light shade of brown. Exposure to the elements would darken it in time.

Higher up, steep slopes had to be negotiated, then a broad, dry shelf. Halfway across the shelf the tracks ended, exactly as if the ground had yawned wide and swallowed the war party whole.

"See, pard," Scott said in dismay. "This is where I lost them."

Nate dismounted and walked in a small circle, contemplating. The ground was hard, but not so hard hoofprints wouldn't show. Where the tracks ended, the soil changed from bare earth to gravel. Ten yards ahead a gravel slope linked the shelf to the high spine.

"Any ideas?"

"Keep your britches on." Nate's circles widened. He kicked at the gravel, noting how loosely packed it was. He picked up some here and there and sifted it in his palm. At the base of the slope he did the same, then ten feet higher.

Scott, still on horseback, was as nervous as a cat in a room full of rocking chairs. "Well, well?" He didn't wait for an answer. "I rode clear to the top and never saw a single print. I couldn't see any on the other side, either. So I got down on my hands and knees and crawled all over this area, figuring there had to be one or two. Yet I couldn't find so much as a scrape." Exasperated, he tugged at his beard. "No one can completely erase sign. Can they?"

"No."

"Then how did this bunch erase theirs?"

"They didn't. They *covered* them."

"They what?"

Nate pointed at the gravel slope. "They spread handfuls of gravel between here and there, then used a tree limb to sweep the gravel over the tracks they made climbing to the top. I suspect they did the same on the other side."

"Handfuls?" Scott said skeptically. "That would take forever."

"Ten men, working fast? No more than half an hour." Nate had to hand it to the invaders. Whatever else could be said about them, they were damned clever. They'd made it appear as if the gravel on the bench was an overflow from the slope. Talus in miniature, so to speak. He was curious to learn if they had used the same tactic on the Utes.

Scott couldn't believe the answer was so simple. "Are you sure?" he asked.

"See for yourself." Hunkering, Nate brushed some of the gravel aside. He only had to dig down half an inch to expose a track. "Satisfied?"

"If that don't beat bobtail." Scott smacked his thigh in annoyance. "I'm a blamed fool for not catching on myself. If I had, I'd have caught up with them by now. Lisa and Vail Marie would be safe."

"Or you'd be dead," Nate countered. "Ten to one aren't very favorable odds. As it is, they're only about five days head of us."

"Five?" Scott said, appalled.

"It's not the calamity you make it out to be. We can catch them before the week is out if we spend twice as much time in the saddle as they do."

"What's today?"

"Monday." Nate wasn't surprised his friend had to ask. It wasn't uncommon for mountaineers to lose all track of time. Calendars were as scarce as hen's teeth, pocket watches and clocks even rarer. The only reason Nate knew what day it happened to be was the almanac he had in his personal library of some forty books.

Scott gazed westward, wringing his hands. "*Another* four or five days? Lordy, do you know what that means?"

"They're not liable to lay a finger on her until after they get to their village. And since they live somewhere beyond Ute country, it could be two weeks before they get there."

"I pray you're right."

So did Nate.

The opposite slope had been brushed clear and gravel strewn for over thirty yards at the bottom. From above no tracks were evident. But where the gravel ended, at the edge of a stand of firs, Nate found hoofprints winding in among the trees.

The trappers forged rapidly on until the middle of the afternoon. Scott complained when Nate called a brief halt for the sake of their horses. He also groused when Nate insisted he eat a strip of jerked venison. But after they were back in the saddle and on the move, he apologized for being so contrary.

The region through which they were passing was one of the most picturesque in the Rockies. Lofty peaks wearing snowy crowns were cloaked in evergreen mantles. Sprinkles of aspens and a few belts of broad-leafed trees lent splashes of color. Lush valleys bisected the mountains, and were in turn bisected by gurgling streams. It was paradise on earth. And it belonged exclusively to the Utes, who had protected their slice of heaven from all outsiders for countless winters.

Some whites were under the mistaken notion that Indians believed the land should belong to everyone. But that was true only to a point. All tribes had certain regions they claimed as their own, and within those regions tribal members were entitled to roam as they saw fit. Let someone from another tribe dare violate their territory, however, and open war would break out.

Most were even less tolerant of whites. They rightly blamed the white-eyes for nearly exterminating the beaver. They had heard about the Mandans and others, whole peoples wiped out by white disease. Was it any wonder, then, that they refused to let a single white man set foot in their domain?

Nate was acutely aware of all this as he rode deeper into the Ute homeland. Two Owls, the only warrior he could depend on to speak on his behalf should they be taken captive, was still far to the north. So while he tracked, he had Scott stay alert for Utes.

Sunset was imminent when Nate drew rein to study the landmarks ahead. All afternoon the tracks had been bearing toward the distant twin summits of a mountain the Indians called Bear Claw. To cross it entailed a long climb to a narrow pass. Taking a calculated gamble, Nate rode on, relying on the war party's tracks until the sun sank into its sheath below the horizon. Once darkness descended, Bear Claw's two spikes guided him. They glowed like faint candles, reflecting the starlight.

Scott Kendall had been unusually quiet for hours. Now he sat straighter in his saddle and placed a hand on the rifle resting across it. "Ever hated anyone, pard?"

"Once or twice."

"I don't mean a mild case. I mean hatred so strong it bunches you up inside like a knot. Hatred that won't let you think of anything except those you hate."

"You're taking this awful personal."

Scott snorted. "Wouldn't you if it was the heart of your heart, the flesh of your flesh? I remember you telling me about the time Apaches stole Winona. You wanted to rip them to shreds, as I recall."

"But I don't recollect hating them. They were doing

what Apaches have been doing since before the Spaniards came."

"So? Does that excuse what they did?" Scott's cheeks were growing ruddy, a sign he was becoming agitated. "Are you going to sit there with a straight face and tell me you didn't hate them? Just a smidgen?"

"I was mad, yes. But hating them would be like hating a grizzly for tearing a person apart. Or a rattlesnake for biting someone who steps on it. That's just their nature, just like it's Apache nature to steal and kill."

"I should turn the other cheek? Is that what you're saying? I know that's what Scripture says we're supposed to do. But—Lord help me—I can't. I just can't. I want to wrap my fingers around the necks of the men who did this and crush their throats to a pulp. I hate them *that* much."

"Remember your promise."

"What? You're afraid I won't be able to control myself? That I'll make a mistake and it will cost us our lives?"

Nate was afraid of that very thing, but he didn't let on. They had a long ride ahead of them, long days of hard travel under hard conditions. Surely, in that amount of time, he could calm Scott down.

If not, there would be hell to pay.

Chapter Seven

"Hellfire and damnation! What the blazes do you mean we haven't been following their tracks for hours?" Scott Kendall was astonished. "Then how do you know which way they took?"

"I'm guessing," Nate confessed.

Scott reined up. They were on the highest slope on Bear Claw, within a stone's throw of the pass that would take them over the range. "And you're the one who claimed *I* wasn't thinking straight! What if you're wrong? It could take us a month of Sundays to pick up their trail again."

Nate clucked to the bay. "Hogwash. All we'd have to do is go back to where they threw you off their scent. It wouldn't cost us more than ten or twelve hours."

"When every second counts, an hour is an eternity," Scott declared. Shaking his head in irritation, he dogged the bay's hooves. "I know you're as smart as a tree full of owls, so there must be a reason you've done what you did."

"If I'm right, I've shaved half a day off the time it will

take us to overtake them," Nate said. The war party made a habit of sticking to game trails, but he had pushed directly for the pass.

"I hope you're right, hos."

"We'll find out soon enough."

The final leg of their climb was done in tense silence. On reaching the narrow defile, Nate halted and climbed down. The ground didn't appear chewed up, as it should. He sank onto his left knee and ran a hand over the soil. His palm made contact with smooth earth—that was all. No gouge marks, no grooves, nothing.

"Any tracks?" Scott asked.

Rather than respond and trigger an outburst, Nate moved closer to the opening. High rock walls reared on either side, plunging the pass into gloom. Leaning the Hawken against the nearest, he dropped onto his hands and knees and commenced to scramble around like an oversized crab, feeling for the prints that *must* be there.

"Oh, no," Scott groaned. "We've lost them, haven't we? This is a fine how-do-you-do! I trusted you, pard. Trusted you to do right by me."

"I played a good hunch."

"That dog won't hunt. Would you have done the same if it were your family?"

Nate was on his feet without thinking. "Now, you hold on," he countered, growing warm under the collar. "Do you honestly believe I'd try harder to find Winona and Evelyn than I would Lisa and Vail Marie?"

Scott squirmed, afraid his rising frustration at being so helpless had made him say something he'd long regret. "No, I'd never do that. You're as true as the Mississippi is wide. I've put our lives in your hands, haven't I? That should prove something."

Nate turned back to the pass and knelt. He had to keep reminding himself that his friend was going through sheer and utter hell. That under those circumstances anyone would be testy. His hand splayed, he groped to the right, then the left. His fingertips brushed a narrow furrow. Examining it closely, he smiled.

"Any luck?"

Beside the first print was another, and another, then a whole jumbled cluster. Nate pried at one with his forefinger and fine grains of dirt crumbled like so much sand. "We're on the right track," he said dryly.

Scott whooped loudly, the cry echoing off Bear Claw and rolling across the woodland far below. "My guardian angel must be watching over us! Keep this up and we'll shave the time it takes to catch those vermin in half."

Going through the pass at night was eerie. Stony ramparts blotted out most of the stars, giving Nate the illusion they were at the bottom of a well. All sound from outside was smothered. All they heard was the thud of their own mounts' hooves, amplified by the close confines.

The air was chill, as it always was at that high altitude. Chill, yet invigorating. Nate had been feeling drowsy, but when they emerged onto an upland bench he was refreshed enough to push on for another hour. The site he selected for their camp was on a wooded spur overlooking the next valley. Pemmican sufficed for their supper, and they went without coffee so their meager supply would last longer. It also spared them from having to make a fire.

Nate was stripping his saddle blanket off the bay when Scott called to him from the edge of the drop-off.

"Take a gander, pard."

To the northwest flickered an orange pinpoint of light. A campfire, three to four miles from Bear Claw.

"Is that them, you reckon? Think maybe they holed up there for a few days before heading home?"

"No," Nate responded bluntly. His friend was grasping at straws. The war party was long gone. Whoever they were, they weren't about to linger in Ute territory after having slain a Ute hunting party. So the fire must belong to one of the Ute bands searching for them. Nate gave his opinion, adding, "We can't let them spot us. They'll badger us with questions, or worse."

Scott patted his rifle. "No one is delaying us if I can help it."

Surrounded by sheltering pines, the two mountain men spread out their blankets and plopped down. Kendall was soon asleep, but Nate lay awake thinking of Winona, Zach, and Evelyn, and how many times their lives had been threatened over the years. *What would it have been like,* he wondered, *if I'd insisted we live in the States instead of in the mountains?* They'd have been safer—but would they be any happier? No, he doubted it. Winona, for one, wouldn't take to being cooped up in a town or city. A farm would be better, but even then she would miss her people and pine for the wide-open spaces.

Zach would fare a lot worse. His mixed lineage would earn him the scorn of every bigot he encountered. He would be shunned by his peers, treated like a leper by those who couldn't be bothered to peer beneath his skin to see the person underneath. Eventually, the resentment he'd pent up would explode in violence. Either he would be hauled before a magistrate or he would flee to the high country, never to return.

Then there was Evelyn. Of them all she would adapt best. Children were much more open and malleable than adults, and as a girl her mixed heritage wouldn't be held against her as severely as it would against her brother. She'd marry a clerk or a lawyer and have a dozen kids, ending her days in a rocking chair on the porch of a house she hadn't left in thirty years.

Nate rolled onto his side. Maybe he had done the right thing, after all. Maybe staying in the mountains, despite the dangers, was best for all concerned. Winona was near the Shoshones, Zach wasn't subjected to as much ridicule and abuse as he would be in civilized society, and sweet little Evelyn had more freedom to choose the life she'd like to live than she ever would elsewhere.

Grinning, Nate closed his eyes. He should be pleased with the decisions he'd made, not plagued by self-doubt. And he should stop dwelling so much on what might have been and dwell more on what could be.

The past was but a stepping-stone to the present, while the present was a gateway to a bright and rosy future. To a time when both his children were married and had kids of their own and he was a happy, doting grandfather, bouncing a gleeful grandchild on his knee.

Wouldn't it be grand?

A jab in the shoulder made Nate sit up in confusion, his hand falling to the flintlocks at his side. A pink tinge framed the eastern sky, and in the nearby trees sparrows and robins were joined in an avian choir.

"Rise and shine, you lazy coon. Unless you aim to sleep the whole day away." Scott Kendall had rolled up his blanket and saddled the buckskin. "I can do without coffee this morning, too, if you don't mind. I just want to be on our way."

"Fine by me," Nate mumbled, struggling to cast off clinging tendrils of drowsiness. He was shocked by his lapse in not hearing his friend moving about and waking up sooner. Evidently he *was* growing lazy, a fatal habit if ever there was one.

As a golden halo adorned the world, they prodded their mounts lower. The tracks steered them toward the south end of the valley, Nate in the lead as before. Several does were scared into frenzied flight, and a squirrel gave them a piece of its mind for disturbing its morning routine. In the tall grass butterflies flitted and insects buzzed. Nate was so intent on reading sign that he didn't give the woods they were approaching much attention. He relied on Scott to keep an eye out for both of them.

"Dog my cats! Is that who I think it is?"

Nate jerked up and spied four riders at the tree line, waiting in deep shadow. He started to raise the Hawken, then saw they were white. The smallest of the four gave a cheery wave, which Nate returned. When he recognized who it was, he wished he hadn't.

Harry Katz was a notorious figure, known all along the frontier as a troublemaker and hardcase. Those he hadn't swindled he had run roughshod over, and rumor had it more than a few of his enemies had wound up with cold steel between their shoulder blades. How he made his living was anyone's guess, thievery ranking high on the lists of those who knew him best. Just the year before, he had been thrown out of Bent's Fort for cheating at cards.

Now Katz plastered an oily smile on his ferret face and exclaimed, "As I live and breathe! The mighty Grizzly Killer himself. Haven't seen you in a coon's age. And lookee who else, boys? It's King's shadow, Scott Kendall."

Nate was studying the other three. They were cut from the same coarse cloth as Katz, dark, cruel men whose natures were indelibly stamped on their grizzled features. One he knew from rendezvous days, a hulking brute of a trapper named Larson. Word had it that when the beaver played out, Larson had hooked up with Katz and the two had been inseparable ever since. "Harry," Nate said coldly, drawing rein.

"Imagine running into you here," Katz said. "Smack in the middle of Ute country. What brings you fellas so far from those cozy little homesteads of yours? Out hunting quail?"

Their dealings were none of the sarcastic ferret's business, and he knew it. Nate wasn't about to say a thing, but Scott let his fear override his judgment.

"We're searching for my wife and daughter. Have you seen them?"

Katz's brow knit. "That pretty filly of yours has gone missing? No, we surely haven't come across the likes of her, or I'd remember." He leaned forward. "What happened? Did the Utes pay you a visit?"

"No, a war party from another tribe," Scott disclosed, and shared the scant particulars.

The ferret and Larson swapped ugly glances. "Let me get this straight, Kendall," Katz said. "You want us to believe that a tribe no one ever heard of was stupid enough to send a war party into Ute territory? And they just *happened* to steal your missus and your sprout? Is that your tale?"

Scott raised his right hand as if taking an oath. "As I live and breathe, it's the gospel. Why would I lie about such a thing?"

Katz snickered. "Oh, I would, if I had ample cause. Mind you, I'm not calling you a liar. That would be dangerous, what with your partner there glaring at me as if he'd like nothing better than to turn me into worm food."

Nate would only abide so much abuse. "Do you really think we'd be loco enough to be here without a good reason?"

"I'm not saying the story you've concocted isn't reason enough," Katz hedged, "but we both know there's a better one. So come clean. We're all white here."

"Suppose you tell us what this better reason is," Nate said testily.

"How about gold?" Katz snapped. "That good enough for you?" His thin veneer of friendliness was fading.

"What gold?" Scott said.

"As if you don't know," said Larson, whose rumbling voice was almost as deep as Nate's.

Scott was confused and it showed. "Know what? Quit beating around the bush and say what you mean."

"Very well," Harry Katz said. "We're talking about the Ute warrior who showed up at Bent's Fort ten days ago with a pouch full of gold. Over two hundred dollars' worth in nuggets. He bought a rifle and trinkets for his squaw, and left." Katz swore a lusty streak. "That damned William Bent tried to keep it a secret. I guess he wants all the gold for himself. But a friend of ours got word to us."

"You're risking your scalps for a handful of nuggets?" Nate said, making no attempt to conceal his contempt.

"Not no measly handful, no," Katz said, greed animating his ferret face. "That Injun told the jasper at the trading post that there's a heap more where those came from. 'A whole mountain of it' were his exact words."

"You're a fool," Nate said.

"Not as big a one as you make me out to be," Harry Katz retorted. "That cock-and-bull story about hunting for Kendall's woman won't float. You're here for the same reason we are. You heard about the gold and you want it for yourselves."

Nate looked at Scott. "We don't have time for this nonsense. Let's go."

Katz placed his hand on his rifle. "Not so fast, King. I'll only say this once. That gold is mine, you hear?" Catching himself, he gestured at his companions. "Ours, rather. And we won't take kindly to anyone trying to steal it out from under us."

Lifting his reins, Nate nudged the bay alongside Katz's buttermilk. "And I'll only say *this* once. We don't give a damn about any gold. If it exists, it belongs to the Utes. And if they catch you, there won't be enough left of your hide to make a parfleche. Savvy?"

The ferret's jaw muscles worked, but he didn't reply.

"We're only interested in Scott's wife and daughter," Nate went on. He was going to suggest that if Katz didn't believe them, Katz should visit Kendall's cabin. But Katz might pay the Wards a visit, too, and cause trouble for Simon and Felicity. "I know I'm wasting my breath, but we'd be obliged if you let us know if you run into Lisa or the girl."

"It'd be a cold day in hell, mister, before I do you any favors."

The remark angered Scott, who balled his left fist and moved his horse forward. "What manner of man are you? You wouldn't help save a woman and a child?"

"Not if they're yours."

Incensed, Scott blundered between Katz and Larson. He didn't see the hulking trapper lunge at him. But Nate did. Unfortunately, he was on the other side of Katz, with

Katz's buttermilk and Scott Kendall's horse between him and Larson. He couldn't bring the bay around fast enough to be of any help, but he could, and did, vault up out of his saddle, pushing off with one hand while his other seized Katz. The ferret emitted a squeal as Nate hurled him to the ground. A quick hop, and Nate was balanced on Katz's saddle, poised to jump.

Larson had grabbed Scott around the shoulders. On seeing Nate unhorse Katz, he released his hold and shifted. The next moment Nate was on him, the impact sweeping them both to the ground.

"Cover me!" Nate roared as his knee dug deep into the other's gut. An arm as thick as a club slammed into his temple, dazing him, and before he could set himself he was flipped onto his belly.

"Give it to that uppity bastard, Zeke!"

A bristling shape towered above Nate. He rolled as a heavy boot stomped down where he had just been. Another roll spared him from harm a second time. Winding up on his back, he saw a black sole arc at his head and grabbed the ankle above it. He wrenched to the left and there was a yelp.

Zeke Larson toppled, clawing at a knife hilt.

Levering up on an elbow, Nate launched himself at the other man before the blade could leave its sheath. They grappled, straining their utmost, Larson hissing like a serpent. Nate had not been in a fight in a while and had forgotten how underhanded mountaineers could be. A knee to the groin reminded him. It sapped his strength, and Larson seized the advantage by locking thick fingers on his throat.

"Kill him! Kill him!" Katz was ranting.

Dimly, Nate was aware that Scott Kendall had brought his rifle to bear on the other three, and that he need not worry about being shot in the back. He bashed his knuckles against his adversary's wrist, but it was like striking solid rock.

Dark eyes ablaze, Larson attempted to clamp his other

hand tight. Nate couldn't let that happen. Twisting and thrashing, he fended Larson off. But it was only temporary. He had to turn the tables or be done in. Suddenly thrusting upward, he smashed Larson in the face. Once, twice, three times, and on the third blow Larson shook like a redwood in a tempest, his grip weakening.

Nate drove both of his legs up and in. They rammed into the bruiser's chest, lifting him clean off. Immediately, Nate pushed partway up off the ground, only to be met by a fist the size of a ham that caught him flush on the cheek.

Katz was livid. "Beat his brains out, Zeke! You can do it!"

Larson tried. He was ponderous but immensely strong, and what he lacked in finesse he more than made up for in sheer brute force. He rained blows on Nate, blows that would have crushed weaker men to crimson pulps. On their knees they fought, slugging it out, trading flurries, jabs, uppercuts.

Nate was rocked, and rocked Larson in turn. He hit Larson's stomach, but the man's abdomen was iron. He flicked two swift punches to the jaw, yet all Larson did was blink. In retaliation, the burly bear tried to butt Nate's face. Throwing himself to the right, Nate landed several powerful wallops to the side of Larson's head.

They were too evenly matched. There was no telling how long the conflict would last. And they never found out. For at that juncture a gun boomed and lead sizzled the air next to Larson's ear.

Scott Kendall, covering the other three with his cocked rifle, had drawn a pistol and fired into the ground. "That's enough," he warned Larson. "I'm not about to have you stave in my partner's skull. He's the only hope my wife and daughter have."

Harry Katz's surprise was the real article. "It's true, then? You're only after your family? Not the gold?"

Scott swiveled his rifle so the muzzle was an inch from the ferret's thin nose. "What does it take to get through to you? Maybe that head of yours can use some ventilation. How about another hole smack between the eyes?"

"You wouldn't."

"Give us any more grief and you'll find out."

Nate was sorry the clash had ended. He felt a peculiar need to pound someone silly, and Larson was as good a candidate as any. Rising, he reclaimed the Hawken and a pistol that had fallen from his belt. His ribs ached, his left ear throbbed, and blood trickled from the corner of his mouth. Licking his lips, he swallowed some. "Another time," he said to Zeke Larson.

"I'll be counting the minutes."

Backing to the bay, Nate mounted and rode into the vegetation. He shifted and trained his rifle on the quartet so Scott could safely rejoin him. Larson, he saw, was slowly straightening and grimacing in pain.

"Don't say I never did anything for you," Kendall said.

"I'm grateful," Nate responded. "Now let's take up where we left off."

Finding the tracks wasn't difficult. Forty-five minutes of steady travel through dense forest brought them to a tableland that could be reached only by a switchback. As they climbed, Nate checked behind them often in case Katz and company were out for revenge.

"Do you believe that nonsense about the gold?" Scott asked out of the blue.

"Why shouldn't I?" Nate rejoined. "The Utes aren't the only tribe to know where some is. An old Shoshone told me once that there are streams where nuggets are as numerous as stars in the sky. You can snatch them right out of the water. No need to pan or work a sluice or anything."

"You never asked him to show you where it is?"

Nate had, in fact, but Winona wanted nothing to do with the yellow ore. She'd heard stories of other whites whose lust for it brought them to grisly ends. "What use would I have for a ton of gold? There's not a lot to spend it on around here."

Scott chortled. "You could always buy out the Bent brothers. Think of it. Your very own trading post."

"For how long? With the beaver trade dying out, they'll be closing up in a year or so." Nate squinted up at half a dozen buzzards. "No, if I had any hankering to be rich, I'd have stayed in the States. How about you?"

"I already am rich. I have the best wife a man could have, and a gem of a girl to raise. A lot of money would be nice, but it's not everything. Money can't buy love."

"Tell that to John Jacob Astor."

Astor, one of the wealthiest men on the planet, owed a large measure of his wealth to being wise enough to exploit the beaver trade when beaver first became the fashion rage of Europe and the United States. He also had the foresight to bail out of the trade once silk replaced beaver, and was now involved in other enterprises.

"I'd rather be happy than rich any old day," Scott declared sincerely. For, as he had learned before coming west, without happiness a man had nothing. In those days he had been stuck at a job he hated, a job where he'd been paid much too little for too much work, putting in so many hours a week he rarely got to see Lisa and Vail Marie. The toll on his well-being had been shattering. He had become moody, his nerves a wreck, always barking at everyone for no reason.

One day Scott simply decided enough was enough. There *had* to be a better life somewhere, and he would go to the ends of the earth to find it. A chance meeting with a trapper fresh in from the Rockies had given him the idea to try life on the frontier. Hooking up with a fur brigade, he'd spent a year gathering plews and judging whether it was safe to bring his family out.

Their new life had been a dream come true. All those years of suffering—and all he'd ever had to do to make his life better was be willing to give up the old and try something new.

Nowadays Scott and Lisa were living as they saw fit, beholden to no one. For over a decade he'd made a fair income as a free trapper. Of late he was dabbling in several areas, serving as a guide to pilgrims on the Oregon Trail, as a scout for the Army, and as a supplier of rare peltries still in demand, such as otter. Alone, the occupations didn't pay that much, but combined it was enough for his family to get by.

Personal needs on the frontier were few. A set of clothes and footwear, a sharp knife, a working rifle, and a good horse were all anyone really needed. People had no use for a closet full of the latest apparel, or enough shoes for every occasion, or fancy carriages to carry them to important social functions. In the States folks were so caught in their craving for worldly goods that they never took a moment to appreciate what really mattered. They never stopped to sniff the lilacs.

Until Lisa and Vail Marie were abducted, Scott had been so happy, so content. Now he was giving serious thought to returning east once they were safe. Secure in his love and his faith, he'd believed that nothing like this would ever befall them. But he had been wrong. And it scared him as nothing else ever had to realize he might lose them forever.

Suddenly Scott saw that Nate had reined up and was gazing back down the switchback. He did likewise and spotted a line of riders at the bottom, just starting up. "I'll be switched. Katz came after us anyway. Do we pick them off from here? Or do it from up top?"

"We ride like hell, is what we do."

"I never thought I'd live to see the day you'd run from a weasel like Harry Katz," Scott remarked.

"We're not running from him."

"But you just said—"

"Those are Utes. And we're too far from our valley for our truce to save us. Unless you want to try and explain what we're doing here through a hail of arrows, we'd best light a shuck."

Scott didn't need to be told twice.

Chapter Eight

Scott Kendall rated himself a good rider. More than good, thanks to spending as much time in the saddle as he did on his own two legs. But he was in awe of his friend, whose ability to race through the densest of growth and over rocky terrain at breakneck speed was little short of dazzling. To say nothing of hazardous.

Scott was given no time to think. He was constantly dodging limbs, continuously ducking out of the way of sharp points thirsting to pierce his eyes, or vaulting obstacles he couldn't go around. The buckskin managed to keep up with the bay, no small feat since the bay was as splendid a horse as Scott had ever seen.

For Nate King's part, he knew that if they didn't outdistance the Utes in the first thirty minutes, the warriors would stick on the trail like glue until they caught up. But he was handicapped by having to follow the same route as the enemy war party.

Not that throwing the Utes off would be easier if Nate could pick any route he wanted. Indians were fabulous riders in their own right. Most were tossed onto a horse almost as soon as they could stand. Some, like the Comanches, virtually lived on their mounts, and could perform incredible feats of horsemanship that had to be seen to be believed.

It helped that the tableland was flat and relatively unbroken except for gullies and a few hillocks. Nate held to a gallop for the first mile, a trot for the second. By then they were at the tableland's western rim and confronted by a talus slope every bit as treacherous as the one that almost claimed Scott's life.

Here, the war party they were tracking had borne to the south, so Nate did likewise. Their tracks paralleled the rim for another half a mile, and more. Nate had still not found where the war party descended when he glimpsed the Utes in the distance, closing swiftly.

"Damn." The delay would prove costly unless Nate found a way down in the next few minutes. As if Providence recognized his need, ahead a ravine slashed the slope, splitting it in two. The south side had buckled, leaving an earthen ramp seventy yards from top to bottom. It wasn't as unstable as talus, but it would be dangerous. Glancing at Scott, Nate grinned. "Are you game?"

"Better game than dead," Scott said, and laughed.

Nate kneed the bay over the edge. The big black balked and had to be kneed again. Over the side they went, the horse locking its forelegs and lowering its rump. Like an oversized sled, it slid down the ramp, gathering momentum swiftly, a fine spray of dust and dirt spewing in its wake.

Scott realized the two horses were too close to each other when the cloud sheathed him in choking particles. Coughing and blinking, he hauled on the reins to slow the buckskin down, but it was sliding as fast as the bay and could no more defy gravity than a rock could.

Scott narrowed his eyes to slits to keep the dust out, but it did no good. They began to tear over, and between the dust and the tears he couldn't see the buckskin's nose, let alone Nate and the bay. Panic surged, but Scott quelled it. They would be all right as long as the bay didn't stop before reaching the bottom.

Up ahead, Nate King saw a small boulder in their path and hollered, "Watch out! Boulder!" Simultaneously, he reined to the right to veer wide. The bay tried to comply, but with its forelegs locked the best it could do was twist at an angle. Nate tensed as the boulder swept toward them. He braced for a collision, but the bay slid past with a hand's width to spare, the boulder scraping the bay's flank. Shifting, Nate looked back to see how his friend was faring.

Scott heard Nate's shout, but the words were muffled by the rattle and hiss of dust and dirt. He swatted at the cloud, seeking to dispel it enough to see, but it was too thick. "What?" he shouted. "What did you say?"

Nate was horrified. He hadn't realized the plight Scott was in, and now it was too late to do anything about it. Or was it? Throwing his whole weight backward, he yanked on the reins to bring the bay to a stop. The horse pumped its rear legs, digging its hooves in deeper, which had the effect of slowing them down. But at the same time, it caused more dust and dirt to gush like a brown geyser at the buckskin.

Scott had no warning. Suddenly the cloud was twice as thick, solid enough to cleave with an ax. So much dust, he couldn't see his mount's head or neck. Tucking his chin, he sought to catch a breath of clean air, but he inhaled more particles. So many particles, they choked him, making him gag. Again Nate yelled, but Scott had no notion what his companion was saying.

Nate was bellowing that the buckskin was almost on top of the boulder. He attempted to turn the bay, but the deep dirt clung to it like quicksand. "Scott! For God's sake! Look out!"

The last two words registered. Scott leaped to a logical conclusion, that he was about to hit something—probably the bay. He wrenched on the reins, but the buckskin wouldn't or couldn't change direction. "No!" he cried, forgetting the dust and paying for his oversight by nearly being smothered.

Seconds from disaster, Nate leaped from the saddle and ran to intercept the buckskin. Or did his best, anyway. Because the loose earth rose midway to his knees, impeding him, pulling at his legs like invisible hands. Every step was a labor. He took four—and it wasn't enough.

Scott felt the jolt of impact, felt the buckskin start to buckle as they were thrown to one side. His left leg spiked with pain. Tugging on the reins, he sought to keep his mount upright, but it was a doomed proposition. The next thing he knew, he crashed toward the ground. Desperation spurred him to push away from the saddle so he wouldn't be pinned, but he wasn't quite clear when they smashed flat. Now it was his right leg that lanced with agony.

Sheathed in dust, they slid downward, out of control, the buckskin on its side with Scott's boot pinned under it. He yanked for all he was worth, but even his seasoned sinews couldn't budge that much weight.

Nate had halted, thunderstruck. Thanks to the dust cloud, he couldn't tell whether rider or mount had been hurt. He ran toward them, only to draw up short when it hit him that they were sliding in his direction. And gaining speed quickly. Backpedaling, he reached the bay and gripped the saddle horn to climb up. He had to get the horse out of there before they were bowled over.

There simply wasn't time.

Nate had one leg lifted to fork leather when, with a sibilant hiss and clatter, the cloud engulfed him. He was knocked breathless by a jarring blow to the sternum. The bay squealed as it was plowed into, and then the world spun and Nate was tumbling and being gouged and scraped and something struck him across the forehead hard enough to nearly cause him to black out.

Abruptly, Nate came to rest on his back. Dirt washed

up over him like water over a beach, covering his legs and midsection. For a moment he thought it would cover his face as well, but it stopped at his neck. Stunned, he lay still. Nearby a horse nickered stridently.

What if one of the animals has busted a leg? Nate slowly sat up, pushing dirt off. The dust cloud was dispersing, but not swiftly enough to suit him. A large shape materialized, stumbling toward him. It was the bay, unhurt except for nicks and scrapes.

"Scott?" Nate called out, becoming alarmed when he received no answer. His head spinning, he forced his body to stand. The sickening sensation faded and he looked around to find the buckskin struggling out from under an enormous earthen pile. It, too, appeared all right. They had been luckier than any two men had any right to be.

"Scott? Can you hear me?" Nate moved toward the buckskin, figuring his friend would be close to it. But Scott was nowhere to be seen. His concern rising, Nate rotated in a complete circle.

Tons of dirt had cascaded down, flowing outward in a wide stream, burying grass and uprooting scrub brush and several small trees. It must also have buried Kendall, Nate realized, and scoured the overflow for sign of a projecting arm or leg.

"Scott! Answer me!" Nate darted to and fro, conscious every second was crucial. His friend would suffocate if Nate didn't reach him in time. He poked into every large mound, into any bump that might conceal a body part, scooping with both hands.

"Lord, no," Nate said, growing frantic. Scott couldn't die! Not like this. Not with Lisa and Vail Marie depending on him.

Nate pivoted, stymied and furious and fit to scream. Then he saw the foot. Or, rather, a single heel, jutting out close to where the slide ended. Dashing over, he knelt and dug. Fingers flying, throwing earth right and left, he exposed a leg down to the knee. It reminded him of the talus mishap. But this time, when he gripped the leg and heaved, he was able to pull his friend out.

Scott Kendall came to with a start. A blow to the head had rendered him briefly unconscious during the chaotic slide. Now a rush of fresh air revived him and he sat up, hacking to spit dirt from his mouth and nose. A strong hand clapped him on the back.

"I thought you were a goner," Nate said.

"You and me both," Scott responded between coughs.

"This makes twice you've cheated death. I wouldn't push my luck and try a third time, were I you."

Scott allowed his partner to boost him to his feet. Running a hand over his scalp, he inspected the gash, pleased it hadn't been reopened. His legs were spongy and his stomach was queasy, but otherwise he was fine.

"We can't dawdle," Nate said, scouring the rim. The Utes could show at any moment. "I'll fetch our horses."

Scot had no objection. He was too weak to do much more than shuffle into the grass and bend over. "I'm still coming, Lisa," he said softly to himself. "Hang on, dearest. Nothing is going to stop me." He prayed that wherever his wife was, she was comforted by the knowledge that no power on Earth could keep him from her.

Lisa Kendall had never been so scared in her life. Yet, strangely, she was also calmer than she had any right to be, given her predicament. Clasping Vail Marie in her lap, she watched the ten warriors closely. They had called a halt a short while before and were huddled together, talking. As usual, they pretty much ignored her. Which suited Lisa just fine. Her great fear had been that one of them would attempt to take advantage, but so far that hadn't happened.

"When will Pa come, Ma?"

Lisa gave her daughter a peck on the cheek. "We have to be patient. It will take some time for him to hunt us down." Of course, trying to convince an eight-year-old to be patient was like trying to stop the rain from falling. It couldn't be done.

Vail Marie plucked a blade of grass and stuck the end in her mouth to chew on. She had never been so unhappy. She missed her father, missed their home, missed her bed and her playthings. She didn't like the bad men who had taken them, and she didn't like being helpless to do anything about it. The only good thing about their ordeal was that she would have a great adventure to share with her best friend, Evelyn, once her pa rescued them.

The warriors uncoiled and spread out, facing the trees. Lisa didn't understand why until she heard the clomp of hoofs. Her heart leapt in the hope it was her husband. But no, the newcomers were coming from the west, not the northeast as Scott would do. She knew this was Ute country, and worried a band of Utes had found them. A fight was bound to break out, with her and her daughter caught in the middle.

But it wasn't Utes. Out of the pines rode two more warriors just like those who had stolen her, leading seven horses. They were warmly welcomed. Another discussion took place, with much gesturing and debate.

Two more of them. Two more to keep Lisa from escaping. She resisted an impulse to curl into a ball and weep. She had to be strong for Vail Marie's sake. And for her own. Should an opportunity arise to slip away, she must be ready. There might be only one chance, and she couldn't waste it.

"Ma?"

"Yes, little one?"

"Will these bad men hurt us?"

Lisa made it a policy to always be honest with her daughter. She was honest now. "I don't know."

"Pa will hurt them, though, won't he?"

"More than likely." Which was putting it mildly, Lisa mused. Her husband was the gentlest man alive, but there were limits to how far he could be pushed. He would tear into the war party like a hurricane into reeds.

"What if we ask them to let us go?"

"They won't."

"Even if we ask real nice? And say please?"

Lisa ran a hand over Vail Marie's hair. "Sometimes being nice isn't enough. There are people who have no regard for how others feel, and will do what they want even if you beg them not to."

"That's not right."

"But it's how things are, and we must make the best of it until your father shows up. I just hope . . . " Lisa gazed off across the valley, biting her lip.

"Hope what, Ma?"

"That he doesn't come alone."

"Why? There are only twelve of them. Samson slew a thousand, didn't he?"

Lisa smiled wearily. Her husband was a deeply religious man. Every evening since Vail Marie's birth, Scott had read to her from the Bible. Naturally, she had taken a child's shine to some of the stories, like the account of Noah and the Ark, and David against Goliath. Somehow or other, Vail Marie had also gotten the idea into her cute little head that her father was as mighty as Samson, that anything Samson had done, Scott could do better. Once, when they were chopping down a rotten pine for firewood, Scott had suggested going for the mule to drag the trunk home. In perfect innocence, Vail Marie had asked him why he didn't just throw it over a shoulder and tote it back as Samson would have done.

"All Pa needs is the jawbone of an ass. Then he can whup these fellas."

Either that or a cannon, Lisa thought. She saw several of the warriors stand and turn toward them.

"Here they come again, Ma. What do they want this time?"

Fear clutching her heart, Lisa pulled Vail Marie closer.

* * *

The Utes were still after them.

Nate had entertained the notion that maybe, just maybe, the warriors wouldn't be foolhardy enough to take the same way down. Maybe, just maybe, they would seek a safer route, which would delay them long enough for Scott and him to make themselves scarce. He should have known better.

Scott had spotted their pursuers over an hour after the two of them had remounted and resumed tracking. They were crossing a row of low hills when Scott bent his head to the side to relieve a kink in his neck and spied the Utes cresting the first hill. "Talk about persistent," he groused. "What now?"

Nate was mulling their options. Too much daylight remained for them to give the Utes the slip. The bay and the buckskin were about played out and would soon need to slow down. So either he tried to drive the warriors off with a few well-placed shots, and brave the wrath of the entire Ute nation, or else he held a palaver and convinced the warriors he had a valid excuse for being in their territory.

Scott was taken aback when his friend drew rein on the crown of the last hill. Doing the same, he wheeled the buckskin and unslung his rifle. "What's it to be? We drop as many as we can before they drop us?"

"We show them empty hands and pray they're peaceable."

Scott fumed at yet another potential delay; each lessened his prospects of saving Lisa and Vail Marie. He had half a mind to drive the Utes off anyway, then realized he had fallen into the same mistake as before. He wasn't thinking straight. Killing just one of them would bring hundreds more down on his head. It might take the Utes a month or a year, but eventually they would extract their vengeance. Thank goodness Nate was along to set him straight! "Empty hands it is."

The warriors slowed a hundred yards out. There were

nine in all, younger men painted and primed for war, bristling with enough weapons to battle an army. In the forefront rode a handsome Ute whose finely beaded buckskins and superb white horse marked him as a man of importance.

"They're itching for a scrape," Scott commented.

Nate placed the Hawken across his thighs and elevated both arms. "Let's not give them cause to scratch."

Against his better judgment, Scott imitated him. "Why do I feel like a lamb about to be slaughtered?"

The warriors were forming into a line, the fancy Ute in the center and slightly ahead of the others. Nate was encouraged by the fact that none had notched arrows to their bowstrings or hiked their lances. He saw no guns. "Let me do the signing," he suggested.

"Be my guest. But make a point of how pressed for time we are."

Head held high, the handsome Ute came to a stop. He stared at the buckskin and the bay, both covered with dirt, then at the two white men.

Nate's fingers flowed. In essence, he signed, "I am Grizzly Killer, friend to the Utes. Friend to Two Owls. My hand is always offered in friendship to my brothers."

Some of the warriors whispered to one another. The handsome one leaned his shield against his chest to free his hands and signed, "We know who you are, Grizzly Killer. All Utes know of you. And of the help you have been to our people. I am Swift Elk, son of Two Owls."

Nate remembered now. He had met the son during the council held by the Utes and Shoshones to settle their dispute over Bow Valley. Swift Elk had been a small boy then. "My heart is happy to see you again. Not four sleeps ago I spoke with your father."

Swift Elk smiled. "He is after killers of my people. So are we."

"They have stolen the woman of my friend." Nate indicated Scott. "We were on their trail when we saw you." He pointed at the tracks, then tactfully signed, "We did not stop to greet you as we should have. For that I am sorry."

"I understand," Swift Elk signed. Sliding off his white stallion, he examined the prints. "This is wrong. My father told me our enemies are twelve in number. I only count ten."

"Maybe the other two were separated from the rest," Nate speculated.

Swift Elk touched a set of prints. "Do these shod horses belong to your friend?"

"Yes. They were taken when the woman and the girl were."

The young Ute rose. "Girl?"

"The daughter of my friend. She has seen but eight winters."

A flush of anger crept over Swift Elk's handsome features. "So these enemies make war on children? I will be glad to count coup on them." Squaring his shoulders, he signed, in effect, "Grizzly Killer, as you are a friend of my father, you are a friend of mine. That you are a friend of my people you have shown again and again." Swift Elk paused as if to choose his next signs carefully. "We have heard many tales of your prowess. How you killed the father of all bears. How the Blackfeet made you run their test of tomahawks and knives, and you survived. How you slew the hairy men who eat the flesh of people. And more."

Nate didn't reply when the younger man stopped. Swift Elk was leading up to something, and Nate had a hunch what it was.

"You have fought our own enemies on our behalf. As your friend, can I do less? If my enemies are yours, yours are also mine. So I hope you will honor us by granting our request."

"What would you have of me?"

Swift Elk looked at his fellow warriors. In the Ute tongue a skinny one said, "Ask him. We are all with you on this."

Scott Kendall was impatient to be off. He was nowhere near as skilled at sign talk as his friend, so he hadn't understood all the young warrior said. Assuming it had nothing to do with their quest, he asked out of the corner of his mouth, "Can't you quit this jabbering so we can move on?"

"Patience," Nate said in English. Then, in sign language, he said, "Finish what is in your heart."

"Your enemies are our enemies," Swift Elk repeated. "My friends and I would be honored if you would let us ride with you against them. We will help you save the woman and the girl. And we will teach these strangers what it means to invade the land of my father and my father's father."

Nate had seen it coming, and he liked the idea. But when he relayed the warrior's request to Scott, his friend hesitated.

"Are you sure we can trust them, hos? They're Utes, not Shoshones. I know I've fed a few when they've stopped at my cabin, but I've never been comfortable when they were around. What's to keep them from sticking steel into our ribs when we least expect it?"

Nate couldn't blame Scott for being uneasy. While the Utes didn't hate whites to the degree the Blackfoot Confederacy did, they hadn't exactly welcomed the white man to the mountains with open arms, either. For years they had tried to drive out Nate's uncle, and later Nate himself. But it was ridiculous to judge an entire tribe by the actions of a few. As Nate had learned, people everywhere were a lot like apples. In every barrel there were green apples, those that weren't ripe, or in the case of people, those who didn't know any better. There were apples ripened to fullness, the same as people whose maturity brought wisdom. And then there were those that were rotten to the core, worthless apples and men alike that had to be destroyed before their rottenness was inflicted on others.

Two Owls's son was sincere, though. Nate would stake

his life on it. "I vouch for Swift Elk," he told Kendall. "But I won't let them tag along if you say they shouldn't. It's your decision."

All the Utes were staring intently at Scott as if they had deduced it was up to him. In their youthful, eager faces he saw no evidence of hostility, only a keen willingness to catch those who had brought so much death and sorrow to their people.

Swift Elk stepped closer and signed at Nate, "Your friend is not pleased?"

"He sees you as he would the Sioux or the Cheyenne. He does not know the goodness of the Ute heart as I do."

In a smooth motion Swift Elk drew his long knife and marched up to the buckskin. Scott automatically dropped a hand to a pistol, then sat there dumbfounded as the Ute reversed his grip and extended the weapon, hilt first. "What's this?" Scott asked.

Nate admired the younger man more by the minute. As the trappers would say, Swift Elk had more horse sense than most, and was a credit to his illustrious father. "He's showing that he trusts you by giving you his knife to stab him with, if you want."

"He'd never let me. It's a bluff."

"Put him to the test. He won't lift a finger to defend himself."

Accepting the weapon, Scott hefted it. The young Ute stood motionless, chest thrust out, braced for a deadly plunge. "I do believe you're right," Scott marveled, observing that the other warriors were as rigid as boards. "Will wonders never cease." Holding the knife by the tip of the blade, he returned it to its owner. "You're welcome to join us, friend. Just save a few heads for me to bash in."

Nate translated, and the Utes yipped like coyotes. Now the chase could resume in earnest. And come what may, they wouldn't give up until Lisa Kendall was safe—or they were all dead.

Chapter Nine

Lisa Kendall was sore and chafed from hours spent crossing some of the most rugged terrain in existence. She was hot and tired and hungry, and incensed that her daughter was forced to endure the same hardships. Vail Marie sat in front of her, holding on to the pommel, bouncing with every step their mount took.

Her abductors were traveling to the southwest at a mile-eating pace. Apparently they were in a hurry to get out of Ute country quickly. Which made Lisa all the more grateful they had let her throw a saddle on her horse before tearing her from hearth and home.

Ever since being taken, Lisa had been trying to figure out who her captors were. She had met Shoshones, Crows, and Utes. She'd seen Flatheads and Nez Percé at the rendezvous. She'd heard descriptions of the Sioux, the Cheyenne, and more. Her captors were none of them.

Little details sometimes told a lot, so Lisa had noted every little detail she could, thinking that it might jog her memory. They were tall and generally stocky, well-muscled and swarthy. Instead of buckskins they wore simple breechclouts and skimpy moccasins. Hardy and stoic, neither heat nor cold affected them. Their language might as well have been Chinese for all she understood of it.

An interesting quirk that Lisa thought might be an important clue to where they were from was that they never used sign language. Granted, among themselves they wouldn't need to. But when ordering her around they always used simple gestures anyone could understand, not the elaborate sign symbols favored by most tribes.

They were armed with knives and war clubs and longbows. Slender quivers brimming with feathered shafts were either slung across their backs or worn on either hip. Their hair was cropped short in front, into bangs that fell to their eyebrows, and longer in back. A few wore necklaces made of shells that Lisa swore had to come from the Pacific coast. But that couldn't be. Surely they hadn't come all the way from California or the Oregon Country!

Lisa reckoned they had obtained the seashells in trade. Few whites realized it, but according to Nate King, Indians had a far-flung network of commerce set up. Tribes up in Oregon, for instance, traded with the Nez Percé and Flatheads, who in turn traded with the Crows and the Shoshones, who in their turn on occasion traded with the Cheyennes and the Arapahos. In that way, a pretty seashell from Oregon might adorn the dress of a Cheyenne maiden, while a buffalo robe crafted by a Shoshone might wind up over the shoulders of a strutting chief somewhere along the Columbia River.

Lisa regretted she wasn't as fluent in Indian languages as Nate. It could help her peg who her captors were.

A husky warrior near the front glanced back at her, his dark eyes betraying no clue as to his sentiments. Lisa had noticed him staring before, several times in the past hour alone. It didn't bode well.

Sunset would occur in less than an hour, for which Lisa was grateful. The war party always stopped for the night, making camp in dense woods or dry washes where they were less likely to be detected. Rabbit or squirrel stew was their usual fare, plentiful game they could kill silently with arrows. She and Vail Marie were both given as much food and water as they wanted, not out of kindness, but in order to keep their strength up. The warriors did not want them slowing the war party down.

Typically, the men were strung out over a hundred yards or better, spaced at thirty-foot intervals. Two husky specimens were assigned to guard Lisa, staying close enough that if she tried to make a break for it, they would catch her before she took three steps. At night the men took turns standing watch in pairs, and although she stayed awake until her eyelids were leaden in the hope they would doze off, they never did.

Another precaution they took was to have a warrior ride ahead of the main group. In the Army that was called riding point, as Lisa had learned from a cavalry officer whose detachment accompanied Scott and her partway to St. Louis.

It surprised her a bit, Indians using sage military tactics. But it shouldn't, she reflected, since Nate King and other mountain men had regaled her with details of Indian warfare. Some tribes were ruthlessly efficient, as organized and skilled as any fighting force ever known.

Suddenly a commotion broke out ahead. Lisa saw the warrior who had been riding point race to the front of the line and have an excited exchange with another. Words were passed back along the line. One of the men guarding her seized the reins from her hand and led her horse into the undergrowth.

All the warriors were taking cover. Lisa was made to dismount and stand behind a wide pine. The warrior pointed at her mouth, at Vail Marie's mouth, then at his knife. The threat was crystal clear. If either of them let out a peep, he would silence them permanently.

Several others had been given charge of the horses and were hastening them deeper into the forest.

The majority were soon well hidden. Lisa saw them nocking shafts to sinew strings and hefting lances. With a start, she realized they weren't trying to hide from an approaching enemy; they were preparing to spring an ambush.

All movement ceased. A deathly hush fell over the woodland. Vail Maire began to fidget, and worried she might say something, Lisa bent low and whispered, "Not a sound or the bad men will harm us."

Vail Marie nodded.

When Lisa looked up, the warrior who had threatened them was glaring at her. He gestured sharply, signifying she must not move or speak again, or else. The long lance in his other hand was poised for flight.

Lisa scoured the country to the southwest. Acres of forest blended into a belt of aspens on the lower slope of a mountain that had to be over ten thousand feet high. Shining snow gleamed in the radiant glow of the setting sun. The scenery was so spectacular, so breathtaking, it was difficult to believe that in another few minutes blood would be spilled.

Off in the trees a horse nickered. The warriors all dropped lower, tense and alert. One of them had climbed an oak tree and was balanced on a limb. His hand moved up and down, a signal of some sort, and he began to extend his fingers one at a time. Four, seven, ten, eleven.

That must be how many riders are approaching, Lisa guessed. Blundering right into certain death.

The man on the limb pressed against the bole.

From out of the pines appeared a horseman. Lisa recognized him as an Ute by his buckskins and his hair. He was absently gazing at the sky, not at the ground. Behind him came others, none with so much as a bow notched. They were tired from a long day of riding, thinking about the camp they would soon make and the meal they would soon eat. They weren't concentrating on what they were doing. They weren't inspecting the ground for tracks or keeping an eye on their surroundings.

Lisa clamped her mouth shut to stifle a warning shout.

Carelessness would cost the Utes their lives, and there wasn't a thing she could do about it.

Suddenly her breath caught in her throat. Lisa had met the third Ute before! She distinctly recalled the gray streaks on his temples. He had stopped at the cabin about five months before, along with a handful of others.

Scott had been away at the time. But Lisa had done as she customarily did and given the warriors some water and food. Going back inside, she had closed the door, thinking that was the end of it. But a minute later someone timidly knocked.

Holding a small pistol behind her back, Lisa had cracked the door to find the one with the gray temples. Smiling tentatively, he'd held out a small beaded pouch, a token of his gratitude. It touched her deeply.

When Scott came home, he was upset. He said she had taken a great risk, that at most she should have gone to the window and signed for the Utes to go away. Lisa did what women always do when their menfolk grumble; she let it go in one ear and out the other.

Now here was that same kindly Ute about to be cut down without a chance to defend himself.

Lisa glanced at the warrior who had threatened her. His attention was riveted to the Utes. A check of the rest showed none was looking in her direction. So, snaking her left hand above her head, close to the trunk, she poked her fingers out the other side and wriggled them. It wasn't much, but it was the best she could do.

The Utes plodded closer, their mounts as tired as they were. Lisa kept waiting for at least one of them to gaze down and see the tracks her captors had made. But they never did.

The warrior who was guarding her turned his head, and Lisa immediately froze. He gave her a suspicious scrutiny, then faced the Utes. She wriggled harder, praying it would be noticed before the trap was sprung.

Eight of the Utes were now in the open.

Lisa felt awful. *They were going to die!* She considered springing toward them and screaming, but the thought of Vail Marie being struck down by a barbed arrow tip or a heavy lance rooted her in place.

Abruptly, the older warrior sat straighter and stared at the tree Lisa was behind. *He had seen her fingers!* To her consternation, he acted more puzzled than alarmed and rubbed his eyes as if he thought he was imagining things. She had to do something else. On an impulse, Lisa showed herself, just her shoulders and head, and slashed a finger across her throat.

The Ute's shock at recognizing her was almost comical. He scanned the trees, lifting his reins to stop, then jerked forward. A shrill cry escaped his lips.

Even as the yell shattered the stillness, the war party attacked. Glittering shafts whizzed, piercing five Utes in half as many seconds. Venting war whoops, the rest of Lisa's abductors burst into the open and let fly with their lances or closed in for man-to-man combat. In a span of heartbeats a swirling melee resulted, with the now outnumbered Utes fighting valiantly for their lives.

Lisa saw the one with the graying hair dodge a thrown lance. He had a war club, which he raised as he smacked his heels against his mount. The horse leaped forward at one of her abductors who was notching an arrow. He lifted his head just as the war club arced down, and it crushed his skull like an overripe melon, brains and gore splattering everywhere.

Men were screaming, howling, dying. Some lay prone, others convulsed in bloody pools. No quarter was asked, none given. Out of the trees swept a Ute with a bow. In the time it took Lisa to step from concealment he put three arrows into as many enemies. Single-handedly he almost turned the tide, but as he was stringing a fourth shaft, a lance impaled him.

In the mad whirl of mayhem and bloodshed, Lisa lost sight of the kindly Ute until his horse appeared from behind another. He was battling two foes at once, one armed with a lance, the other wielding a club. They fiercely attempted to topple him, but he fended them off with sweeping blows.

The Ute evaded a thrust lance tip, shifted, and lunged, slamming his club onto the shoulder of his assailant. Then, as fluid as water, he swung around and crashed his club into the face of his other foe, who had bounded in close.

Momentarily in the clear, the kindly Ute glanced at Lisa. He started to goad his mount toward her. To save her and her daughter, Lisa realized, her heart leaping for joy. She dared to believe he would swing them on behind him and they would escape. But it wasn't meant to be.

The kindly Ute was halfway to the trees when an arrow transfixed his right shoulder and nearly knocked him off. How he clung on, Lisa would never know. But he did, and as he righted himself more enemies converged to finish him off. He shot Lisa a last look, a look of regret and dismay that tugged at her heartstrings. Her spirits sank as he did what he had to—namely, he wheeled his horse and rode for his life.

He was the only one to get away. The rest of the Utes were down, some alive but too severely wounded to lift a finger against the triumphant war party, which had little to celebrate. Four of their own lay in the grass, lifeless, and three others had been hurt.

It had all happened so incredibly fast. Lisa was dumbfounded. She'd never witnessed anything like it, never seen so much blood shed in so short a time. Unconsciously, she was holding Vail Marie's face pressed to her bosom so her daughter couldn't see the carnage.

"Ma—?"

"Hush. Be still."

Lisa thought the worst was over, but she was mistaken. The victors dragged five Utes who were still breathing to a clear spot and placed them side by side. The tallest warrior, the one she took to be the leader, drew a knife and stood over one of the wounded men. She figured he would slit the poor Ute's throat and that would be that.

The tall man bent low, taunting his victim, who was in such agony from a head wound, he didn't appear to hear. Smirking, the tall man drove his blade into the Ute's belly, burying it, and the Ute arched his spine, opening his mouth wide to scream. But no sound came out. Even when the tall warrior methodically commenced to slice from right to left, shearing through flesh and internal organs as if they were mush, the Ute never cried out. Spittle frothed his lips and convulsions seized him.

Lisa wanted to tear her gaze away but couldn't. Her horror turned to loathing when the tall warrior slid his fingers into the cut he'd made and yanked out a thick ropelike strand of slimy intestine. Bitter bile rose in Lisa's throat and she had to swallow to keep from being sick.

Some of her captors were laughing at the Ute's expense. Their laughter grew louder when the tall man wrapped the intestine around the Ute's neck and proceeded to strangle him with his own guts.

The barbaric spectacle repulsed Lisa. Rotating, she stalked off, whispering to Vail Marie, "Don't look! Whatever you do, don't look!"

Footsteps pounded. A hand fell on Lisa's shoulder, and she was spun around. The man who had been guarding her gave her no hint of what he had in mind. He simply hauled off and slapped her across the mouth. Rocked on her heels, Lisa staggered against a tree. The man hiked his hand to hit her again, but he grabbed her arm instead and hauled her to the small clearing.

The torture was continuing. One man was chopping fingers off the Utes, another toes. A third was making a collection of ears, while a fourth was involved in an act so unspeakably vile, Lisa couldn't bear to watch.

"Ma? What's that fella doing?"

Lisa had forgotten about Vail Marie. Twisting from

the warrior's grasp, she put her back to the horrid scene. "I told you not to look! Listen to me when I tell you what to do!"

"I'm sorry, Ma."

Upset that she had vented her anger on her daughter, Lisa hugged Vail Maire and kissed her cheek. "I'm sorry, truly sorry. But there are some things it's better you don't see or they'll torment you the rest of your days."

"I wish Pa was here."

So did Lisa. More than anything else in the world, she yearned for her husband to fly to their aid before the same thing that had happened to the Utes happened to them. Lisa now knew her captors were capable of the most wicked atrocities imaginable.

It filled Lisa with dread. Maybe they hadn't stolen her to be the wife of one of their warriors. Perhaps they had another, more loathsome fate in mind. For her, and her sweet daughter. Overcome by emotions too long contained, unable to fend off tears any longer, Lisa bowed her head and quietly wept.

Vail Marie squeezed her mother's shoulder. "It's all right, Ma. Don't you fret. I'm here to protect you."

Lisa Kendall cried as she had never cried before.

The two mountain men and their Ute allies settled into a routine. Up at the crack of dawn, on the go before sunrise, they would ride all day, stopping briefly now and again to rest their horses. Nightfall didn't deter them from forging on, though it did slow them down. They adopted Nate's tactic of fixing on distant landmarks their enemies were headed toward, and not stopping until they reached them.

They pushed themselves for eighteen hours out of every twenty-four, with only one meal to sustain them. After two days Nate was sore and tired, minor inconveniences he shrugged off.

Usually Swift Elk rode beside him, and between sign language and Nate's smattering of the Ute tongue, they became well acquainted. The young warrior had ambitions typical of warriors everywhere. He desired to become a man of renown, like his father, to count many coup, own many horses, and marry a certain lovely who had caught his eye. He valued honor above all else, and would rather cut out his own tongue than tell a lie. His sole weakness was his pride.

Swift Elk believed his people were better than any others, nobler, finer, more perfect. Ute men were braver warriors than the Sioux, the Comanches, the Piegans. Ute women were more beautiful than women anywhere. He also took enormous pride in himself, in his appearance and his prowess. He had a small mirror he'd obtained at Bent's Fort, and Nate lost count of the number of times he caught the young dandy admiring his own reflection.

But for all that, Swift Elk was a personable fellow, ready of wit and humor. He was also every bit as tough and true as he liked to say he was.

The rest of the young men seemed in awe of Nate. At night they'd pester him to tell about his exploits. Of all white men, only the "Blanket Chief," as the Utes called Jim Bridger, was more famous.

Scott Kendall rarely spoke. He had withdrawn into himself. Every waking moment, he struggled against a flood tide of anxiety and despair that clawed at his soul. His wife and daughter were all he thought about, all he cared about. Each day he'd forget to drink and eat unless reminded by Nate. At night he lay under his blanket with his eyes closed, but he was lucky to get an hour's sleep. His mind wouldn't shut down. Worry encased him like a cocoon.

Scott found himself reminiscing a lot. About meeting Lisa for the first time, and how smitten he had been by her charm and her intelligence. About the birth of Vail Marie, the single greatest experience in his whole existence. About the joys of having a family.

His fondest memories were of ordinary things. Lisa dusting the cabin, Lisa hanging out clothes, Lisa, with an apron around her waist, butchering a grouse for supper.

Vail Marie, playing with her dolls. Vail Marie, dashing gleefully around the cabin, a sprite in her glory. And best of all, Vail Marie at bedtime, when he would tuck her in and she would give him a hug and kiss him on the cheek. Those were the moments that made life worthwhile.

Thus preoccupied, Scott was the last to become aware of a dozen or so buzzards circling ahead. Only when Nate nudged him did he look skyward. So many vultures together was rare. Scott recalled seeing it only once before, after a surround conducted by the Shoshones, when more than seventy-five buffalo had been slain. Hot fear spiked through him, and he urged his horse into a trot.

"Wait for us!" Nate hollered.

Scott would wait for no man. Not when those ugly carrion eaters might be circling over Lisa and Vail Marie. Heedless of limbs that tore at him, he took the straightest course, crashing through whatever barred his path. The racket he made would forewarn whoever might be up ahead, but he didn't care.

More buzzards were on the ground, congregated around dark forms sprawled at random. As Scott drew near, the vultures took ungainly wing, flapping loudly. So did a cloud of insects, buzzing upward in a writhing black mass. *Flies!* So many, they had blackened the bodies they covered.

Swatting to shoo them off, Scott reined to a halt. A foul odor assaulted him, a stench fit for a charnel house, a stink that churned his stomach. Covering his mouth and nose, he went from corpse to corpse, seeking his wife and daughter. What he found were Utes, butchered and bloated and left to rot in the sun.

Nate King and Swift Elk were next on the scene, Nate spying a warrior who had endured the anguish of the damned. The man's eyes had been gouged out, his nose and lips hacked off, sharpened stakes driven into his limbs to pin him to the earth. Hideous as that was, compared to some of the others, the man had gotten off lightly.

The remainder of the young Utes arrived, and were as stunned as Swift Elk. He had dismounted and was stumbling among the dead as if he were almost dead himself. The handsome young warrior's face was a mask of disgust tinged by growing outrage. At one of the fallen figures, he cried out. Falling to his knees, he went to place a hand on the man's ruptured, festering flesh, but stopped at a shout from the skinny Ute.

Nate was watching Scott Kendall closely. His friend made a circuit of the area, then stood with tears streaking his cheeks. "What's wrong?" Nate asked, walking over.

"They're not here."

"I should think you'd be glad."

"I am."

"Then why the tears?"

"Joy. Pure joy."

"Ah." Nate motioned at a log. "Why don't we light a spell? It'll be a while before we can ride on."

Scott's legs were as weak as a newborn's, his knees like pudding. Wobbling like a foal taking its first steps, he reached the log under his own power and planted himself. As he wiped an arm across his face, Nate's statement sank in. "What? Why can't we?"

"The Utes will want to tend to their dead. It could take the rest of today and most of tomorrow."

A rush of indignation restored Scott's vigor. "I can't wait that long and you know it! We'll have to go on without them. They can catch up later."

"We can use their help, pard."

"Be reasonable. You can't expect me to sit here twiddling my thumbs while the bastards we're after spirit my family farther and farther away." Scott screened his eyes with a hand so he could note the position of the sun. "It's almost noon now. In another half an hour I cut out whether anyone comes with me or not."

Nate had anticipated as much. "Don't go off half-cocked. Let me work some jawbone medicine with Swift Elk."

"Palaver until you're blue in the gills. I'm leaving regardless." Scott watched his friend move off and frowned. Being curt with Nate went against his grain, but he couldn't help himself. The warriors who had Lisa were to blame for the slaughter, and the abominable deeds they had committed could just as well have been done to Lisa or Vail Marie. From now on, he couldn't slack off for a single minute. As hard as they had been pushing, he must push harder. God willing, in another two to three days he would overtake the fiends and the nightmare would end.

Scott saw Nate hunker beside Swift Elk. *Why wait,* he asked himself, *when every second is so vital?* Standing, he sidled toward the buckskin. Nate's back was to him, and the Utes were busy with their dead.

No one saw Scott grip his mount's reins. No one looked around when he slowly ambled off on foot, leading it past other horses left unattended.

Scott paused a few times to give the impression he was stretching his legs. One of the warriors gazed at him, so he smiled. The Ute was too downcast to return the favor, and turned to a companion.

Another ten feet and Scott was in the pines. His saddle creaked under him as he climbed on, then glanced at Nate King one last time. *Goodbye, old friend,* he thought. They had been through a lot together, stood shoulder to shoulder against impossible odds. Nate would be mad at him for running out on them, but he had it to do. Something deep inside was spurring him on, and it would not be denied.

Scott Kendall flicked his reins and rode off to confront his destiny.

Chapter Ten

"How do you think your pa is faring?" Louisa May Clark asked.

Zach King paused in the act of swinging back his arm to hurl a flat stone. "Pa? I reckon he's doing just fine. Why do you ask?"

They were on the west shore of the lake, the water as still as the air, the surface a polished mirror reflecting their images. The two of them were standing close to one another, Lou with her hands clasped behind her slender back. "Oh, I don't know. I figured you must be worried."

"About Pa?" Laughing, Zach threw the small stone and grinned as it hopped like a grasshopper. "Six times! The best I've done today. Let's see if I can do seven." He bent to find another.

This was one of those times when Lou didn't know what to make of him. Were it her father, she would be worried sick. She mentioned as much, adding, "Don't get me wrong. Your pa is as strong and brave as anyone I've ever met, but even he can die. I don't understand why you're not gnawing your nails over whether he'll make it back."

Zach stopped searching. "Sometimes you just beat all, you know that? You make it sound as if I don't care because I'm not thinking about him every minute."

"I never said that," Lou responded, bewildered by the accusation. "All I'm saying is that you never seem to fret about him much, and that doesn't seem normal."

"So now I'm addlepated?"

Lou placed her hands on her hips. "Stop putting words in my mouth. What's gotten into you? Can't you answer a simple question without being so darned defensive?"

Zach had never seen her so mad at him before. "What's gotten into me?" he countered. "You're the one acting like a badger with a burr stuck to its butt."

"Why—why—" Lou didn't quite know what to say, she was so incensed. And hurt. Here they were, having their first spat, over something so silly it hinted that maybe her life wouldn't be all peaches and cream when they became man and wife. That scared her. A lot.

Feeling regret, Zach gave her a hug and kissed her lightly on the lips. Usually that was enough to bring a smile to her face. But she was looking at him as if he were someone she had just met. "What? What did I do?"

Lou tried counting to ten in her head. Her ma always claimed that worked when her pa was being particularly dense.

"Of course I'm worried," Zach said. "But I don't dwell on it. Besides, Pa has tangled with hordes of Blackfeet, Bloods, and Sioux, and always gotten the better of them. He'll come riding up here as big as day anytime now."

While Lou found Zach's confidence in his father admirable, she thought he was taking it a mite too far. "No one is invincible. That includes your pa. I pray you never have to find that out the hard way."

Zach felt that *she* was the one being unduly hard, and he was about to tell her so when his sister came skipping out of the trees. Rather than direct his anger at Lou, he directed it at Evelyn. "Where the blazes have you been? You've been gone for pretty near half an hour, and ma told you to stick close to us."

The youngest King wasn't intimidated one bit. "You've got it backwards. As usual. Ma told *you* to stick close to *me*. Which you didn't do."

"You're the one who ran off," Zach said defensively.

"No, I told you I wanted to go for a walk in the woods. But you didn't want to. You wanted to stay here and make cow eyes at your sweetie."

At moments like this, Zach was sorry his parents ever had another child. "We're going back now," he announced. *And good riddance to both of them.* He would saddle his dun and go for a ride. A long ride, to give Lou time to cool off.

Evelyn grinned. "Don't you care to hear where I went and what I did?"

"No." Zach started for the trail to the cabin.

Maybe it was to spite him, or maybe Lou was sincerely curious, but she said, "Well, I do. What have you been up to, little one?"

It annoyed Evelyn, a girl who wasn't all that older than she was calling her "little one." But she had such a tremendous secret to share, she overlooked the insult and replied excitedly, "I found a cave."

Zach halted. "You did not."

"Did to."

"You're making it up to trick us." Zach knew how his sister thought. "You're hoping we'll traipse around the woods with you for an hour or so, then you'll tell us the whole thing was a big joke and laugh yourself silly."

Evelyn wondered why God ever saw fit to invent brothers. "I'm serious, Stalking Coyote."

Folding his arms, Zach pondered. She never used that tone or called him by his Shoshone name unless she was sincere. And he recollected a story told by Touch the Clouds, to the effect that in the old days there *were* several caves in the valley but the Shoshones had sealed them up. "Where did you find it?"

Pointing northward, Evelyn said, "Yonder. I felt some cold air blowing on me. And when I looked, I found this big hole in the ground. And saw the little man."

"The what?"

"A little man sitting down in the cave. He was all brown and dried up, like a berry that's been in the sun too long."

Lou was fascinated. "Really? Goodness gracious. Was it an Indian? Did he say anything to you?"

"No, I think he was dead. He didn't move or anything. He just sat there, smiling like he was happy to see me."

"Take us to him."

Zach had heard enough. "Lou, you can't be serious. She's pulling our legs. There's no cave, and even if there is, there sure isn't no little man. She's making the whole thing up. Trying to convince us she saw a NunumBi, when anyone with half a brain knows there are no such people."

"A NunumBi?" Lou said.

Evelyn squealed in delight and clapped her hands. "The NunumBi! Of course! Why didn't I think of that? The little people who live in the mountains and shoot their little arrows into folks!"

"They do what?" Lou was beginning to agree with Zach. His sister was fabricating a tall tale to make them look silly.

"It's an old Shoshone legend," Zach explained. "Older than any Shoshone can remember. About the days when dwarfs and giants and wild creatures bigger than our cabin roamed the land. The giants were supposed to be ten feet tall, and carried clubs no ordinary man could lift. There were birds as big as buffalo, called Thunderbirds, because when they flapped their wings it sounded like thunder. No one takes the stories seriously." He gave Evelyn a pointed stare. "At least, no one who is grown up."

"Touch the Clouds and Drags the Rope told me the

NunumBi are still around," Evelyn held her ground, "and they'd never lie."

"Could it really be?" Lou said, stirred by accounts her own grandparents had related of life in the old country, of the fair folk and pixies and leprechauns and the like. It astonished her the Indians had their own version of the Little People.

"Now who's acting addlepated?" Zach asked, wondering how she could take his sister's nonsense seriously. "If the NunumBi exist, then elk can fly." Chortling, he hiked toward the high trees. "Come on, you two goofs. Ma told us not to be gone too long."

Lou's cheeks acquired a pink hue. "Men!"

"Brothers!" Evelyn declared.

The two girls stared to the north, then the older grasped the younger's hand and they headed for home. The mysterious cave, with its mysterious occupant, would wait to be explored another day.

Nate King was mad enough to spit glowing coals. Mad at himself. He should have seen it coming, should have realized his heartsick friend's torment would lead Scott to do something rash. Now here he was, racing like a Chinook wind to catch up and stop Scott from doing something rash.

Beside the bay trotted Swift Elk's splendid white stallion. Four other warriors were with them. The rest had stayed behind to make sure the slain warriors were properly sent into the hereafter.

Swift Elk wasn't the same man he had been before finding the bodies. Gone was his smile, his outgoing nature, his willingness to gab. He was a dark and terrible shadow of his usual self, ominous lightning crackling in his eyes. He had signed only one statement to Nate in hours, and that was when they mounted up to go after Kendall. "My people will be avenged. This I vow."

All the Utes were equally somber, equally subdued.

Their thirst for vengeance ruled them to the exclusion of all else.

By Nate's reckoning, Scott was an hour and a half ahead, or better. He hadn't noticed his friend was gone for the longest while, and when he did, he'd assumed Scott had ventured into the trees to heed Nature's call. The truth didn't hit him until he saw that the buckskin was gone, too. By then Scott had a forty-five-minute head start. Getting the Utes to make up their minds about who would stay and who would go had taken another quarter of an hour.

Now here they were, driving their weary horses anew, their urgency compounded by Nate's need to save Scott from himself.

As time went by and it became apparent they weren't going to overtake Kendall anytime soon, Nate fell into a funk of his own. He would hate to lose Scott. He could count the number of truly good friends he had left on one hand. Life in the wilderness took a savage toll on those audacious enough to live there. Many of the trappers he had known were pushing up clover. Many close friends had met ghastly deaths at the hands of hostiles or under the slashing claws of ravening beasts.

It had always been thus. In the early days of the beaver trade, hundreds of young men flocked to the Rockies in their bid to emulate John Jacob Astor. Most did well enough at first, earning up to a thousand dollars or better at the rendezvous. This in a day and time when the average laborer in the States was lucky if he made four hundred dollars a year.

The money never lasted long, however. Supplies at the rendezvous cost three to five times as much as they would in St. Louis. And unless a trapper wanted to travel clear across the prairie, wasting weeks of valuable time, he had no choice but to make the best of a barely tolerable situation.

What little profit the mountaineers made usually went

for foofaraw for the maidens, and whiskey. Trappers were powerful fond of drink. Strong drink. The kind that curled the hairs on a man's chest and curled his toes in rigor mortis if he wasn't careful about how he conducted himself while under the influence.

Then it was off into the mountains again, for two more seasons of trapping before the next rendezvous. Usually it was there, in the remote fastness of the peaks, in the solitary pursuit of their chosen trade, that so many lost their lives.

Shakespeare McNair once estimated that of the two to three hundred men who were at the rendezvous in 1830, less than a handful were still alive ten years later. Nate thought the number was more, but he had no means to verify who was right. Many mountaineers gave up within the first year and went back home without telling anyone, others had gone on to California and the Oregon Country, and some took to living with Indians, becoming adopted members of a tribe and forsaking all their white ways. But it was safe to say the death toll had to be high. Scores—if not hundreds—of bleached skeletons littered the vast expanse from the Mississippi to the Pacific.

Nate King didn't want Scott Kendall's bones to be among them.

The buckskin showed signs of flagging toward evening, but Scott didn't slacken his pace. Either the horse held up, or it didn't. And if it gave out he would find another somehow, someway.

It felt good to know that from here on out he wouldn't let anything hold him back. Scott raised his face into the wind and smiled. *I'm sorry, Nate,* he thought. *Hope you won't hold it against me, partner.*

Another day was almost done. Scott wasn't going to stop, though, until close to midnight. He wasn't worried about losing the trail, as he'd done that first day. The tracks were plain enough for a greenhorn to follow, and he was no greenhorn. Besides, the war party was making no attempt to conceal their sign. They were in a hurry to put Ute territory behind them.

Scott intended to catch them before they did. From what he'd heard, the land beyond was unexplored and inhospitable. A burning wasteland, rumor had it. A land where those the boiling sun didn't bake alive, hostiles staked out on anthills. Even those bold adventurers, the Spaniards, hadn't penetrated very far.

Scott shuddered to think of Lisa and Vail Marie enduring such an ordeal. As capable and strong of spirit as his wife was, she had never been faced with so severe a challenge. She'd never been tested to her limit of endurance, and beyond.

Then there was Vail Marie, so small, so young, so fragile.

Gazing at the heavens, Scott asked the same question he had posed dozens of times in the past few days. *Why us, Lord? Why did you let this happen to a God-fearing family like us? What have we done to deserve to be punished so?*

The answer, of course, was nothing. Absolutely nothing. They were decent, peaceful folk who never harmed a soul unless set upon. Lisa and Vail Marie were innocents who'd never committed an evil deed in their whole lives. They didn't deserve this.

Why, then, indeed? Scot mused. The only answer was that "things happened." Man had no more control over the events of his day-to-day life than he did over the weather. No one was the master of his own fate. Oh, many liked to pretend they were. They set themselves up in a good-paying job and bought a nice home and owned the latest carriage, and in their arrogance they thought they had the world by the tail. But they were oh-so-wrong.

The simple truth was that man was a leaf in a gale, a twig in a stream, driftwood on the ocean. People were swept along by currents they couldn't see, much less comprehend. And sometimes those currents churned through rapids, where if a person wasn't careful they would crash onto the hard rocks of grim reality.

It was a bitter lesson to learn.

Especially at the cost of a wife and daughter.

Lisa Kendall was exhausted. Not so much physically as emotionally. She felt drained, utterly drained, and she was gladder than ever when the tall warrior indicated a ridge they were approaching and said the same words he always did when it was time for them to stop for the day.

The ridge would overlook their back trail. Extra vigilance on the part of her captors, who were more careful than ever since ambushing the Utes.

Lisa had learned a few things about them since the bloodbath two days before. To begin with, the purpose of their raid was to get their hands on all the horses they could gather up by hook or by crook. That became evident when she saw the fuss they made over the Ute animals they had caught. Two almost came to blows over a fine sorrel each wanted.

Some tribes, like the Blackfeet, ranked stealing horses high on the list of deeds that earned warriors coup and prominence. The Sioux, too, were accomplished horse thieves. They loved their warhorses so much that when enemies were sighted in the vicinity of a Sioux village, the warriors brought their best horses into their lodges at night to safeguard them.

Lisa had also learned who her captors were, at long last. It happened during a short rest that very afternoon, when the tall warrior who led the war party came up to her and squatted. Pointing at his chest, he'd said, "Ammuchaba." Thinking it was his name, she'd pointed at her own. "Lisa."

The leader then pointed at Vail Marie and arched his eyebrows.

Lisa told him her daughter's name and was surprised when the man motioned as if to say she had misunderstood. She arched her own brows.

Again the man pointed at himself and said, "Ammuchaba." Swiveling, he pointed at another warrior. "Ammuchaba." At a third. "Ammuchaba."

"It's the name of your tribe?" Lisa had responded, knowing full well he didn't know English from Greek. Ammuchabas? A name she'd never heard.

Smiling, the leader pointed at her once more and waited.

Amazement set in as Lisa realized he wanted to know what her people were called, not what her name was. *The Ammuchabas had never seen a white person before!* Flabbergasted, she'd gawked at him as if he were from another planet. Gawked so long that he grew annoyed and pointed at her again, sharply this time, his brows pinching in anger. "I'm a white woman," Lisa had blurted. "White."

"White?" He'd said the word tentatively, rolling it on his tongue as if he were tasting it. "White. White. White." Content, he had gone off.

The third lesson was that her captors had no mercy whatsoever. Or precious little.

Yesterday morning, shortly after they started out, one of the wounded men fell from his mount and couldn't get up. It was the man whose shoulder had been splintered by the gray-haired Ute's war club. The wound was grievous. Bone had burst outward, shredding skin, and the Ammuchaba had lost more blood than Lisa deemed safe.

Nothing his companions tried staunched the flow, so that first night two of them held him down while a third applied a burning brand to the shoulder. The stricken warrior had been given a stick to bite down on, but he still cried out.

The blood stopped flowing, yet the man became weaker and weaker. He was listless, always running a fever, and refused to eat much. Finally the ravages took their toll and he'd fallen from his horse.

Lisa expected the others to help him back up. They'd

tie him on so he wouldn't slip off again and be on their way. But they had other ideas. A short talk between the leader and several others ended with one of them drawing a knife and sinking the blade between the man's ribs. They gave no warning. They didn't consult with him. They just up and killed one of their own, and the warrior who performed the foul deed claimed the man's horse as his own.

Lisa could rationalize why they had done it. Their companion was too far gone and would only slow them down. But to kill him outright like that! It had been so cold, so calculated, giving her whole new insight into their character.

It also reaffirmed Lisa's decision not to do anything to antagonize them. To them she was a novelty, the first white woman they had ever seen. They were taking her to their village as a trophy of sorts, to show their people the strange person they had stumbled across. But that was all she was to them. A curiosity. It made her dispensable, and giving them sass might be all it took to provoke them into slaying her.

"Ma, I'm awful tired," Vail Marie piped up.

Her daughter had been so quiet for so long that Lisa thought she must be dozing. Easing her forearm, which was curled around her daughter's waist, she responded, "So am I. But in a short while we'll be stopping and you can get all the rest you need."

"It looks like Pa isn't coming today. Do you think tomorrow he will?"

Vail Marie had asked the same question daily since they were taken, and Lisa always had the same answer. "We'll have to wait and see. I'm sure he's doing all he can."

"I hope nothing happens to him. What if Pa has an accident and can't catch up to us?"

The same secret dread kept Lisa awake nights. She didn't fancy the notion of spending the rest of her days penned up in a lodge as the wife of an Ammuchaba. Or maybe one of several wives. Some tribes, she'd heard, practiced polygamy.

"Will we stay in the mountains after this is over?"

Lisa hadn't given it any thought. But what *would* they do once—or, rather, if—they were rescued? Knowing Scott, he'd be all fired up to take them back to the States where it was safer. He'd blame himself for their abduction even though he had been miles away. For all they knew, if he *had* been home he'd be dead now. The war party might've killed him to get to her.

"I hope we do," Vail Marie was saying. "I like it here."

"In the States you could go to school. Have a lot of friends your own age. And you'd never need to worry about hostile Indians or grizzlies or painters."

Vail Marie twisted to bestow a loving gaze. "I just want to be with Pa and you. You pick where and I'll be happy so long as I'm with you."

Statements like those were every parent's treasure. Lisa kissed her on the head. "I hope you feel the same when you're eighteen and married. I'd hate to end my days with no grandchildren to tickle and spoil."

A shout by the leader brought the war party to a halt. Soon the horses had been tethered, guards posted, and two men had tramped into the trees in search of game. Lisa and Vail Marie were left in the watchful custody of the man who had slapped her the other day.

Holding her daughter, Lisa walked to a spot where she could see for miles to the north. In the fading sunlight the mountains were splashed with vivid colors, Nature in all her royal glory.

"What's that, Ma?" Vail Marie asked.

"What's what?"

"See that mountain way, way off? The one with just the top showing? What's that on it?"

Lisa had to peer intently to make out the distant figure. "I wish I had your eyes." Something, an elk or black-tailed deer, maybe a bear, was swiftly descending a high slope. It was so tiny, it appeared to be an ant. "Could be anything."

"Think it's Pa?"

The idea hadn't occurred to Lisa. Suddenly her heart leaped and her intuition flooded her with the conviction that, yes, it really and truly *was*! But she hoped she was wrong. For it meant he was alone, and by himself he was no match for the Ammuchabas. In his haste to save them, Scott was rushing headlong to his death.

Darkness fell while Scott was still high on a range. The buckskin was breathing raggedly and caked with sweat. By rights, he should stop before it keeled over. But he refused. Another day, two at the most, and he would be with his wife and daughter. Nothing was going to stand in his way.

Then the buckskin lurched. Scott had to fling his hands against its neck to keep from being thrown. It tottered as if drunk, drool foaming the bit, and slowed on its own accord.

"No!" Scott reined up. "Not now! Not when I'm so close!" Climbing down, he examined it and a rare oath escaped him. The buckskin was on the verge of collapse. Either he stopped for the night now, and let it rest until morning, or in another hour it would give out completely and he might as well put a lead ball into its brainpan.

This can't be happening! Scott railed, raising his face to the sky in mute appeal. At that instant, golden shafts of sunlight radiating from the setting sun shimmered above him like Heaven's pearly gates. It had to be an omen, he thought. A sign that if he didn't lose faith in his Maker, his Maker would guide his steps.

Others wouldn't agree with him. Other people might see only the sunlight and not think to look beyond the sunbeams to their source. But Scott knew. He just knew.

Bolstered by newfound confidence, he walked the buckskin into a patch of firs and made a cold camp.

"I'm coming, Lisa. I'm coming" were Scott's last words to himself as he slipped into a fitful sleep, while lower down on the inky mountain wolves howled as if in feral lament.

Chapter Eleven

There had been another delay, the third in five days.

First a mistake by one of the Ammuchabas was to blame. The war party had stopped at a meadow to rest the horses, and as was their routine, a warrior was given the task of watching over the two dozen animals acquired on their raid. The man sat with his back to a tree—and dozed off.

No doubt he thought it was safe to relax. The horses were tied together in three strings of eight each. But that didn't stop them from running off when one suddenly whinnied and bolted. Whether it had been spooked by a snake or caught the scent of a predator, Lisa never knew. All that really mattered was that its panic was contagious, and within seconds all the stolen horses were racing away.

The warrior leaped to his feet, but the harm had been done. Immediately, the rest of the men jumped on their mounts and gave chase. Some had witnessed his lapse. Most, as they rode past, struck him with their quirts or lance butts. The man didn't resist. Head bowed, he stood and took his punishment in stoic silence, even though by the time the last of his companions rode off, his face was covered with welts and cuts and blood.

It took five hours to round up the horses. Some had broken off from their strings and gone their separate ways. Three were never found. When the war party came back, the tall leader gave the man whose neglect was to blame a severe tongue-lashing.

The second delay was due to a rock slide. They were winding along a narrow ledge that would bring them to the top of an escarpment when they came to a section that had been washed away by a recent rock slide. They had no recourse except to retrace their steps. But with the ledge no wider than the length of their bows, they couldn't turn the horses around. They had to dismount and walk the animals down *backward.* Some, naturally, balked. It took two hours, and then they lost another two finding a new way to the top.

The third delay was that very morning, and Lisa herself was to blame.

They had risen at first light and resumed their journey before the sun was halfway up. Since the previous afternoon dense forest had hemmed them in, giving the illusion they were adrift in a sea of pines. By sticking to a game trail they made good time. Deer and elk used it daily, which was a sure sign it would eventually bring them to water.

Lisa rode with Vail Marie perched on the saddle in front of her, ducking low limbs and avoiding branches. Glancing back, she noticed that the warrior behind her had fallen a dozen yards to the rear. The man ahead was almost as far. They were lax because they didn't think she would try anything, not with near-solid walls of vegetation on either side. But those green walls only *appeared* to be solid. There were gaps, openings, plenty of places a horse could slip into and be gone in the blink of an eye.

Lisa wavered, though.

Were she alone, she would try to escape in a heartbeat,

but she had her daughter to think of. An arrow meant for her could strike Vail Marie. And even if none did, what if they were caught? Their punishment might be worse than that of the man who let the horses run off.

Those horses.

The evening before, Lisa had seen the tall leader and two others admiring an Ute mount, a magnificent chestnut with white splotches on its flank, and white socks. On their way back to the fire they had passed her, and the leader paused. He had indicated the stolen stock, pumped his arms and body as if he were riding, and beamed like a small boy given his heart's desire for his birthday. Then he'd said the name of his people and some other words in their tongue.

Lisa was puzzled what to make of it. Was he saying that riding a horse was one of his greatest delights? Or that all Ammuchabas were passionate horsemen, as devoted as the Comanches?

Unbidden, another idea blossomed. Lisa had seen how the warriors handled themselves on horseback. They weren't exceptional, by any means. Average, was how she'd rate them. Which seemed inconsistent if they were anything like the Comanches. Unless—and here she was stretching logic, but it explained a lot of things—unless they were new to the horse, unless they were just starting to collect valuable breeding stock, unless their excursion into Ute territory was the first they'd ever made.

It wasn't that far-fetched. Many tribes had acquired horses within recent memory, mainly thanks to the Spanish. And mainly those tribes that lived to the south, along the border with Mexico, who later traded some with those who dwelled on the plains. Indians deep in the interior weren't as fortunate; many didn't have horses to this day.

It accounted for why she had never heard of their tribe. Granted, she wasn't as knowledgeable about Indians as Nate King or Shakespeare McNair were. But she'd spent many hours in the company of those two gentlemen, regaled by their stories of life in the wild. At one time or another they'd talked about every tribe under the sun. Yet not once did either ever mention the Ammuchabas.

When all was said and done, where they came from was of little consequence. Getting away from them was all that should concern her, and Lisa knew she would regret it for the rest of her life if she failed to seize an opportunity when it presented itself.

Like now.

Drooping her shoulders and head as if she were so tired she couldn't sit straight, Lisa shifted just enough to see the man behind her out of the corner of an eye. He was fifteen yards back and acting as bored as a tavern owner at a Sunday sermon. The warrior in front was watching a pair of squawking ravens.

Ahead, a bend in the trail materialized.

Lisa bent down to whisper. "Vail Maire. This is important. Don't say anything or look at me. Just hold on tight, tighter than you ever have. I'm going to try and escape."

Nodding, the child molded herself to the pommel.

Lisa gripped the reins securely and scoured the vegetation on both sides. On the left was a thicket in the shadow of large pines. On the right the undergrowth wasn't as heavy, which worked in her favor since she could ride faster. But she'd be easier to spot, too, and thus a lot easier to hit.

Which way should she go?

Lisa didn't make up her mind until the very last second. Plodding around the bend, she verified that the warrior to the rear couldn't see her, and that the one in front wasn't watching.

As if heaven-sent, an opening presented itself on the right. Without breaking stride, Lisa rode into it and smacked her heels against her mount to spur the animal on. She needed to put several trees between them and the trail before the warrior following her came to the bend.

No outcries rent the forest. No shrieks of outrage. Lisa grinned and dared to think she would pull it off, that it would be minutes yet before they noticed she was missing. Flicking the reins, she cantered deeper into the woods. They covered another thirty feet.

"You did it, Ma!" Vail Marie said quietly.

Lisa was marveling at how easy it had been when a strident yell crushed her newborn joy. Bringing the horse to a trot, she sped for their lives.

To the rear, the brush crackled to the passage of many riders. Shouting back and forth, the warriors were swiftly spreading out.

Vail Marie tilted her head. "Don't let them catch us, Ma. Please don't let them catch us!"

Lisa tried her best. She called up all the riding skill she possessed and galloped flat out, tucking at the waist to shield her daughter from rending limbs. To throw off their pursuers, she veered to the right and fifty yards later veered to the left. Not surprisingly, Lisa lost track of where she was in relation to the game trail. She thought she was heading north, but it could just as well be east or west. Her sense of direction was askew.

"Ma! Look!"

Lisa glanced in the direction her daughter was pointing. Angling toward them was a husky Ammuchaba, fury wreathing his head like a storm cloud. Cutting sharply away, Lisa was horrified to spot another coming from the other side.

"There's one more, Ma!"

They had caught up so swiftly!

Lisa choked down welling frustration and applied herself anew. So long as breath animated her, she mustn't give up. Not for her sake alone, but for the sake of the child whose life was more precious to her than the most exquisite diamond in the world.

"Here come others!" Vail Marie wailed.

Lisa heard them, plowing through the forest like living scythes. Oddly, they didn't whoop and holler as Indians were wont to do. They were in deathly earnest, as grim as the grave.

The woods were a blur, the vegetation a jumbled quilt-work of greens and browns. Everything flashed by Lisa in the blink of an eye. She had to react instantly as obstacles presented themselves. Logs. Boulders. Low limbs.

It was one of the latter that did her in.

For frantic minutes the chase lasted, Lisa holding her own but unable to shake the Ammuchabas. She had to keep track of where they were, hold on to Vail Marie, be on the lookout for perils in her path, and control her horse, all at the same time.

Try as she might, Lisa couldn't look in all directions at once. She had two eyes, not forty. And it was when she checked over a shoulder to gauge how close her captors were that the inevitable took place.

"Ma!"

Vail Marie's scream whipped Lisa around. Directly ahead was a thick limb that hung so low, it would barely clear their mount's head. Lisa bent lower, but she couldn't bend far enough with Vail Marie there. Nor could she lean to the side, not when it would expose her daughter to potential harm.

Deliberately, Lisa bore the brunt of the impact. She expected it to be severe but not the bone-jarring, gut-churning blow it was. Bodily torn from the saddle, overwhelmed by agony, she hung in the air for what seemed like a full minute but couldn't have been more than a second. Then she smashed to earth and heard hoofs pound and her daughter scream.

"Vail Marie!" Lisa cried, struggling to stand. Her traitor legs wouldn't obey. She did manage to rise onto her knees, and she lifted her head just as the tall leader bore down on her like a centaur gone amok. She saw him spring from his horse before it stopped moving, saw him rear over her with his fist cocked.

An inky veil descended.

Scott Kendall held warm coals in his hand and almost kissed them. They proved he was hunkered before the campfire his wife's abductors had made the night before. The war party was only several hours ahead.

"I'm coming, dearest," Scott declared as he anxiously climbed on the weary buckskin. "Another day, horse," he told it. "Then you can take your sweet time going home, and rest up all you want."

The trail wound into dense forest. Giddy with joy now that the end of his quest was nigh, Scott goaded the flagging buckskin on at a pace that threatened to cause it to collapse. He reckoned it would be the middle of the afternoon before he came within sight of the war party, so he was stupefied when, well before noon, low voices warned him he was much closer than he figured.

Now isn't the time for mistakes, Scott reflected. Reining up, he advanced on foot, avoiding fallen leaves and dry twigs, exercising the stealth of a painter. Movement steered him toward a clearing on the bank of a stream. He was so excited, blood hammered his temples and his chest was fit to burst. He could hardly wait to set eyes on his loved ones again. It took all his self-control to keep from calling out their names.

Someone spoke, close by, in an unknown dialect. Scott promptly flattened and saw two pairs of moccasins off to the left, along with dozens of hoofs. Crawling to a thorny bush, he carefully parted it wide enough to see two dusky warriors standing guard over tethered horses. Beyond were more men, some drinking from the stream, some talking, one man applying a whetstone to a knife blade.

Where were Lisa and Vail Marie?

Scott's breath caught in his throat as his worst fear surged rampant. Had they been killed? Was he too late? After all he had gone through, after all they had endured, to think that they were gone was almost too much to bear. Suddenly he stiffened.

Across the clearing were his wife and daughter. Lisa had been tied to a tree and was slumped forward, her disheveled hair hiding her face. Vail Marie was also bound, but on the ground. His little girl was weeping.

Simmering rage gripped Scott. He resisted its pull and dug his fingers into the soil as if to hold himself down. Then Lisa lifted her head and he saw dry blood and a discolored knot on her cheek and his rage became all-consuming. Of their own accord his legs pushed up off the ground and hurtled him into the clearing.

It was hard to say who was more surprised, Scott or the warriors. One of the sentries spun and hiked a lance, but Scott cored the man's brain with a lead ball. Drawing a pistol, he fixed a bead on the other warrior and was thumbing back the hammer when corded arms encircled him from behind.

Like a griz gone berserk, Scott heaved his assailant off, pivoted, and squeezed off a shot. The bullet slammed into the warrior's shoulder, not the heart as Scott intended. He shoved the spent flintlock under his belt and reached for the other, but as he unlimbered it, feet pounded and someone hissed like a serpent.

Three more were almost on top of him. Scott brought the pistol up, but the man he had just shot was as tough as rawhide and grabbed him around the shins. Kicking wildly, Scott fought to free himself and succeeded just as the trio reached him.

A war club arced, smashing against the flintlock and sending it flying. Scott still had the rifle, which he gripped by the barrel while evading the war club's next swing. He rammed the stock into the warrior's midriff and, when the man doubled over, cracked him across the skull.

Every last Indian was converging. Scott waded into them, blind to everything except his need to batter, to bash, to destroy those who had dared violate all he held dear. He clubbed those in front, he clubbed those on either side, he clubbed them as they tried to circle to get at him from the rear.

The *thud-thud-thud* of the stock connecting with human flesh was punctuated by the whoops of the warriors. One notched a bow and trained an arrow on him, then lowered it at a bellow from the tallest among them. From then on, they did their best to close in so they could grapple him to the ground.

They wanted him alive! That much sank in, that much pierced the red haze of bloodlust that had Scott in an unbreakable grip. He swung the rifle in a frenzy, again and again and again, never resting, never tiring, driven by an inner force he couldn't resist.

Across the clearing, Lisa Kendall saw her husband battling to reach her side. Her heart swelled with love such as she had never known, love so potent it brought a lump to her throat and blurred her vision with tears. Fully half the Ammuchabas were down, writhing and clutching themselves, while the rest swarmed like hornets around a bear, around her man, striving to bring him to bay.

An inarticulate cry of dismay was torn from Lisa when the rifle was ripped from Scott's grasp. She thought they had him now, that he would be overpowered and brought down, but Scott balled his big fists and drove into them anew, punching in fiery abandon.

Lisa had never beheld him like this, never seen him caught up in the heat of combat, never suspected he was capable of such carnage. He was frightening, yet wonderfully magnificent. Because he was battling for *her,* for her and their daughter, and nothing short of death would stop him.

Belatedly, Lisa spied a warrior with a war club slinking toward Scott from behind. "Look out!" she screeched, but he couldn't hear her above the din. Surging against her bounds, Lisa pulled and pried in a futile bid to rush to his side.

The warrior raised the club. Lisa screamed her husband's name, but he didn't look. He was slugging it out with four others at once when the club slammed into him.

Pain was relative. Just when a person thought they'd experienced the worst torment there was, along came anguish that made all previous suffering pale into insignificance.

The pain in Scott Kendall's head reminded him of this basic truth when he drifted up through a clinging gray fog and was abruptly fully conscious. Agony pummeled him like falling boulders, and he grit his teeth in order not to be unmanly.

Disoriented, Scott opened his eyes. He was on his side, his hands tied behind his back, another rope closing off the circulation to his feet. Levering onto a shoulder, he raised his head for a look-see.

"Pa! You're alive!"

Scott shifted on an elbow. Incredibly, his pain evaporated like dew under a blazing sun when he set eyes on the pair with whom his heart was entwined. He saw them, and only them. The tender love in Lisa's eyes, the tears pouring from Vail Marie, they were a soothing balm for his tortured soul. He yearned to enfold Lisa in his arms and kiss her until his lips wore off, and to toss Vail Marie into the air and whoop for glee.

"I knew you'd come!" his daughter said. "I've been telling Ma the whole time."

Scott's gaze devoured his wife as a starving man devoured food. "I thought I'd never—" he began, and couldn't finish.

"Me, too," Lisa said, putting more affection into those two words than many wives expressed in a lifetime.

Such was the depth of their devotion that for a while neither spoke. They merely looked into each other's eyes, communicating in a way that made speech unnecessary. They would have gone on doing so had not their offspring wriggled and sat up, asking, "What do we do now, Pa? How do we get out of this fix?"

Scott tore himself from Lisa. The warriors were huddled beside a small fire. Although it was early yet, they appeared in no hurry to move on. On the contrary, half were busy trimming and sharpening limbs already chopped into two-foot lengths. *Stakes,* Scott realized, a chill coursing through him. "I'm sorry," he said softly.

"For what Pa?" Vail Marie asked.

"Yes, why?" Lisa said.

"I failed. I've let you both down when you needed me most." Now that his berserker fury had faded, the full import of what Scott had done filled him with remorse. His blunder would cost his family their lives.

Vail Marie's cherub features were streaked with grime and her dress was a shambles, yet to Scott she'd never appeared more sweet and adorable than when she wriggled closer and said, "Don't talk like that, Pa. You'll get us out of here yet. Just break those ropes like Samson would."

Scott closed his eyes and groaned.

"Is Pa sick, Ma?" Vail Marie asked. "Or is he hurting from all those bruises?"

A shadow fell across them, and Lisa glanced up. The leader of the war party was glaring at her husband. She mustered a wan smile, but it was wasted. Since her escape attempt, the man treated her with scorn.

Fingers closed on Scott's shoulder and he was roughly thrown onto his back. He stared up into the quartz eyes of a warrior almost as big as Nate. "What's your problem, hos? Come to stomp on a gent when he's down?"

The leader squatted. Leering, he nodded at the stakes being whittled, then at the center of the clearing.

Other warriors were bringing dead wood and piling it. To what end was a mystery, but Scott guessed it had something to do with him, and that he wouldn't like what it was. "Do you speak Shoshone?" he asked in that tongue. "Or Crow?" He'd mastered enough of both to trade or parley when he met roving bands.

The leader reached for Scott's possibles bag. He jerked away, but he couldn't prevent it from being stripped off and upended, the contents spilling out.

Vail Marie pumped her legs at the warrior but couldn't

quite reach him. "Stop that! You give my pa's things back!"

"Hush!" Lisa snapped, not meaning to. She was intensely afraid the Ammuchaba would backhand Vail Marie, or do something worse, which would incite Scott and result in both of them being hurt. "Don't antagonize them. We need to keep our wits about us."

Scott had been about to kick the man himself. Sagging, he gnashed his teeth in baffled wrath as the warrior sorted through his belongings. The pemmican merited a sniff. His small folding knife elicited a grin when the man figured out how to open it. But the objects that garnered the most interest were his fire steel and flint. "Just help yourself, why don't you?"

The warrior ran a hand over the fire steel, then the flint. Their purpose was not hard to divine, and he struck them together. At the sparks it produced, he smiled and stood, crowing about his sensational find.

"I'm glad someone is happy," Scott quipped, and Vail Marie giggled. She was so naive, so innocent, he shuddered to think of her fate if he couldn't pull a miracle out of thin air.

"Are you alone?" Lisa gave voice to the question that had plagued her for days. "Please tell me you're not. Please tell me others are with you, and are out there waiting for the right moment to move in."

By Scott's best estimate, Nate and the Utes were half a day away. No help would come from that quarter, and Scott had not seen any sign of other Utes, either. "We're on our own," he said. "Come what may."

"Ma?" Vail Marie said. "Why do you look so awful sad? Don't cry. Pa will teach these men to let us be. Wait and see if he doesn't."

The pile in the center of the clearing was already waist high and growing. One of the warriors toted an armful of stakes over next to it.

Lisa refused to think of thc possible use they would be

put to. Smiling warmly at Scott, she said softly, "Do you remember when we first met? I dropped my hymnal and you picked it up for me?"

"You were the prettiest girl in the choir." Scott would never forget that day as long as he lived—which might not be much longer. "I'd always been fond of you, but I was too scared to tell you."

Vail Marie tittered. "You, scared? Oh, Pa, you're like Samson. You're never afraid of anything."

Scott didn't set her straight. Why bother, when in a short while she would learn the truth. Once the torture commenced. To his wife, he said, "The proudest day of my life was when you took me for your husband. To this day, I can't believe that a wonderful woman like you cares for a guy like me."

"Scott Kendall, you're the kindest, most decent man I've ever met. I'm the one who is honored. And I want you to know that I don't regret a minute of our life together. Not a single, solitary minute. If I had it to do all over again, I'd still gladly be your wife."

Vail Marie was squirming. "Anytime you want to break those ropes is fine by me, Pa. I'm tired of being tied up."

The tall leader barked commands. Four strapping warriors hustled to Scott and seized his arms and legs. He resisted, but he was powerless against their combined might. Vail Marie screamed and flung herself at them, but the toe of a moccasin flipped her aside as if she were a kitten.

Lisa didn't rail at their captors, or cry. She was beyond that point. Emotionally, she felt drained, numb. She saw them bear her husband to the middle of the clearing, saw the leader pick up a stake and raise it as if to plunge it into Scott's chest. Her beloved was about to perish and there was nothing she could do.

Or was there?

Chapter Twelve

Nate King had never ridden a horse into the ground. He didn't treat his mounts as if they were disposable, like some men were inclined to do. He never abused a horse, or beat one, or let one come to harm if he could help it.

There were times, however, when necessity forced Nate to push an animal much harder than he ordinarily would. Times when lives were at stake. When swiftness was paramount no matter what the cost.

This was one of those times. Nate rode the bay to the brink of collapse in his zeal to overtake his friend. He felt sorry for the animal, but he dared not slacken his pace. He held the lives of three people in the palms of his hands, and he refused to fail.

Swift Elk and the Utes never complained. They kept up, driving their war horses as mercilessly as he did the bay. Their thirst for vengeance would not be denied.

Exhausting mile followed exhausting mile. Grueling day followed grueling day. The toll on men and mounts was formidable. Humans and horses alike had to reach deep down within themselves for extra stamina. They had to tap into the reserves of the life force that animated them.

But strive as Nate would, he couldn't catch Scott Kendall. A few hours always separated them. A few measly hours, yet it might as well be an eternity.

By the tracks, it was evident the buckskin wouldn't last much longer. The day before, Scott had halted briefly, and the poor buckskin hadn't moved once. It had stood in the spot where it stopped, ignoring green grass all around, and a nearby spring. Added evidence the animal was at the end of its rope.

Nate envisioned the buckskin caked with sweat, head hung low, tongue lolling and sides heaving. It had always been a reliable packhorse and he'd rather not lose it, but by the time he caught up with Kendall it might be beyond salvaging.

Yet another day dawned, warm and sunny. Nate stiffly clambered into the saddle, yawned, and headed out. The temperature climbed rapidly. Soon he was uncomfortably hot. As he skirted a hogback, Swift Elk appeared at his elbow and signed to him.

"In two sleeps, Grizzly Killer," was the English equivalent, "our enemies will reach Corn Creek. Once past it they are out of our territory and in their own."

"Will you chase them that far?"

"I would gladly do so," the handsome warrior replied, "but my father said I am not to do so unless he is with me."

Which was wise of Two Owls, Nate mused. Younger warriors tended to think they were invincible, to commit acts seasoned warriors would never contemplate. Just a year before, he'd heard about a bunch of young Blackfeet who tried to steal horses from the Sioux. Rather than lie in hiding and wait for the herd to be driven out to graze, they'd brazenly snuck into the heart of the village in the dead of night and been slaughtered to a man when a barking dog gave them away.

Youthful zest was intoxicating and treacherous. That

tingly, vibrant feeling of being alive lent to the belief that such would always be the case. Death was something that happened to others. But the young died as frequently as the old, the only difference being that the old tended to wither away like a fading plant, while the young burned themselves out in a blaze of misspent glory.

Nate often fretted that such would be the case with Zach. Stalking Coyote was as hotheaded as they came, and took risks Nate never did. But then, Nate had been reared in New York City, where the greatest daily danger he'd faced was crossing streets jammed with speeding carriages.

Swift Elk coughed, and Nate realized the young Ute had signed to him and he had missed it. "Yes?"

"What will you do if they cross the Corn, Grizzly Killer?"

"I will go on. I will hunt them to the Great Water if need be."

"Then we will ride with you. My father will understand."

Unending acres of woodland unfolded before them, lush virgin forest like that which once existed east of the Mississippi. Were the situation different, Nate would take time to drink in the natural splendor. Now he had eyes only for the tracks he dogged, which brought him to a game trail that meandered into the depths of the woods.

Nate didn't like having vegetation press in so close. It was ideal for an ambush. Yet he did not slow down. Butterflies flitted by like gaily-hued fairies. Bees buzzed from flower to flower, chipmunks chittered and birds chirped. It was a wonderland, the wilderness at its best. The creatures were proof that no one lay in wait, that the rhythms of nature had not been disturbed.

Then, miles into the forest, the wild things vanished, the chirping died, the sounds of all life faded as if blinked out of existence.

Nate drew rein, his senses primed. Either a silvertip was abroad or something had driven the animals into hiding. Based on the tracks, he wasn't more than a few hours behind Scott. Twice that behind the war party. So they weren't to blame unless one or the other had unaccountably stopped.

A while before, Nate saw where a shod horse had left the trail and was hotly pursued. Lisa had made a bid for her freedom, he gathered, but been recaptured.

At a walk, Nate continued on. He feared Scott's butchered body might lie around every turn, just as he had feared finding it each and every day. But there were only tracks, tracks he knew as well as his own by now.

"Grizzly Killer!" The whisper, in Ute, brought Nate to another stop. He rotated in the saddle.

"I hear voices," Swift Elk signed.

Rising in the stirrups, Nate turned his head from side to side. Other than the sluggish breeze rustling leaves he heard nothing, and he was about convinced the young Ute was mistaken when he heard them, too. Faint, but unmistakable.

Without being told, the Utes dismounted and girded for combat. Nate checked the Hawken and both pistols, adjusted his powder horn so he could grab it quickly, then loosened his knife in its sheath.

They were as ready as they would ever be. Nate assumed the lead, gliding on cat's feet, as quiet as a stalking bobcat. The voices grew in volume, the tongue completely unknown to him. Off through the trees a group of men were gathered in the center of a large clearing. Nate saw horses, some on the near side, some at a stream. He could not quite make out what the warriors were up to. They were gesturing and laughing as if at a joke.

A hand fell on Nate's arm. Swift Elk extended a finger to the left, and Nate saw Lisa Kendall, tied to a tree. Little Vail Marie was at her feet, trussed up like a lamb about to be delivered to the butcher.

"Where is your friend?" Swift Elk signed.

Nate wished he knew. Scott should be there somewhere, unless he had circled around and was spying on the war party from the other side. Then Nate spotted the buckskin, lathered to a froth and worn to the point of buckling. Another few steps, and the mystery of Scott's whereabouts was solved.

The warriors ringed a pile of firewood high enough and wide enough to serve as a bonfire. It struck Nate as odd that they would build a fire during the hottest part of the day. But it wasn't to keep them warm or to use as a signal. It was a pyre. Only, in this instance the person to be burned was still alive.

Scott Kendal had been staked out spread-eagle, the wood placed *on top* of him. From his ankles to his beard he was entirely covered.

A tall warrior squatted. Sneering, he held out a fire steel and flint where Scott could see them. Then, tearing handfuls of grass out by the roots, he wadded the kindling between a couple of limbs.

They were fixing to burn Scott alive! Nate counted seven, several of whom were wounded. One appeared to have a fresh gunshot hole in his shoulder. That made the odds exactly even. Turning to Swift Elk, he signed instructions.

As the Utes crept off, Nate sank onto his belly and snaked toward Lisa and Vail Marie. His plan was simple enough. While the Utes attacked the invaders, he would cut mother and daughter loose. Once they were safe, he'd get Scott out of there. It should all be over in a matter of minutes.

But Nate wasn't halfway to the females when the tall warrior with the fire steel and flint stuck them together over the kindling. Within seconds the grass ignited. A few puffs by the warrior and the tiny flames swelled into larger ones that ate at the dry wood with horrific quickness. A third of the pile seemed to go up at once.

It changed everything. Scott would die before Nate reached him unless something drastic was done. The

Utes weren't in position yet, so it was up to Nate. Flinging himself into the open, he wedged the Hawken to his shoulder and let out with a Shoshone war whoop.

Lisa Kendall had spotted the mountain man and his allies but had not let on for fear the Ammuchabas would notice. She had thought to distract them by raising a ruckus, but when Nate and the Utes separated, she concluded they must have a plan of their own and it would be better if she followed their lead.

Then the tall warrior lit the firewood, and Lisa's heart stopped. Vail Marie screeched like a banshee. It galvanized Lisa into renewing her attempt to loosen her bounds. A lost cause, but she had to do *something*. That was her husband who would soon be charred to the bone!

Scott Kendall had always been a fair hand at cards. He could hide his emotions with the best of them, and he did so now, hiding his apprehension as the tall man hit the fire steel against the flint. In slow motion Scott saw the sparks fly into the grass, which burst into flame. He took a breath to try and blow them out, but the wily warrior had placed the kindling too high up.

Of all the ways Scott had imagined meeting his Maker, being roasted like a buffalo haunch wasn't one of them. He surged upward, but he couldn't rise an inch. Held fast by the stakes, he'd suffer agony the likes of which no one should ever endure. He could only hope the sweltering heat caused him to pass out before the flames seared his body.

The tall warrior was smirking at him, relishing what was to come. Scott tried to collect enough spittle to spit on his tormentor, but his mouth was too dry. So he contented himself with saying, "Were you born a polecat, or have you worked at it? Too bad I won't be around to see you get your due."

The tall man's smirk widened, then disappeared as a loud cry rent the clearing. A cry Scott Kendall had heard before. The last time had been when he tangled with some Sioux, alongside Nate King.

Twisting, Scott beheld his friend sprinting from cover and raising the Hawken.

The war whoop had the desired effect. It diverted the attention of the seven warriors, but it also gave them a split second to react before Nate fired. And to a man, they dropped to the ground just as the rifle discharged. The lead intended for the tall one whizzed above his head.

Instantly, the war party was up and charging, even those who were wounded. War clubs and lances were hoisted. But as the Ammuchabas attacked, out of the forest hurtled the Utes, Swift Elk at the forefront. The two sides crashed into each other like two bulls in rut.

It was man to man, weapon to weapon, sinew pitted against sinew, reflexes matched against reflexes.

The Ammuchaba who had shown so much interest in Lisa closed on Swift Elk. Both were armed with knives. They feinted, thrust, circled, taking the measure of each other. The older Ammuchaba thought he saw an opening, and his blade darted like the tongue of a rattler. But Swift Elk was aptly named. He sidestepped, lunged, and cut the Ammuchaba's upper arm.

All this Nate took in at a glance. He had gripped one of his pistols, but in the rabid swirl of battle he risked hitting an Ute by mistake, so he didn't shoot. Then, above the melee, rose a child's cry.

"Pa! Pa! Nooooooo!"

Nate pivoted. The tall warrior had turned toward Scott. Whipping out the pistol, Nate raced to his friend's aid. He took aim, but a pair of battling warriors filled his sights and he had to slant to the right to go around them. By then the tall warrior had his knife high overhead for a fatal stab.

"Me! Try me!" Nate bellowed. The tall man looked around, and Nate snapped off a shot. Or tried to. The gun misfired, spewing smoke but no lead.

All the tall warrior had to do was finish his stroke and Scott was finished. But apparently he had little or no experience with firearms. At the spurt of smoke, he recoiled, then spun on a heel and bounded for the trees.

Nate reached the pyre. Sliding his knife out, he sank onto a knee and slashed the rope that bound Scott's left wrist. So far only the upper layers of wood were burning. His friend had been spared from the worst of the awful heat. "I'll cut the other one," he said, starting to rise.

"No! Give me the knife and go after him!" Scott responded. "I can get out of this on my own!"

Nate didn't like the idea.

"We can't let him get away! Go!" Scott insisted. "He's their leader. He might come back again one day. Lisa and Vail Marie will never be safe as long as he's alive."

"Here!" Nate shoved the hilt into his friend's hand and barreled into the brush. Scott had a point. If any members of the war party made it to their own land alive, the Kendalls, the Wards, and Nate's own family were in danger. He had to catch the tall man and end it, once and for all.

Scott Kendall had thought it would be easy. He would reach across, cut his other wrist loose, and push off enough firewood for him to stand. But when he tried to reach the other stake, the mountain of branches on his chest and shoulders hampered him. He couldn't quite do it. So, setting down the knife, he began to throw the limbs off.

Meanwhile, the flames were burning lower, steadily lower. His buckskins were so hot, they could erupt in flame at any time. Sweating profusely, he grit his teeth and kept throwing, throwing, throwing.

As if Scott didn't have enough to worry about, smoke now billowed from the pile. And with no wind to disperse it, a thick roiling cloud was slowly sinking toward the bottom. He grabbed a large branch and flung it, shoved another, flipped a third. Yet, as fast as he worked, it wasn't fast enough.

Scott inhaled deeply a moment before the acrid cloud enclosed his head. It blinded him, stinging his nostrils even though he wasn't breathing. He groped at the wood, scattering some with a powerful sweep. But not enough. For when he reached across to see if he could touch the other stake, it was still out of reach.

Bracing his free hand under him, Scott levered himself, trying to sit up. He could rise only five or six inches. And when he did, searing flames nearly singed his face. His eyes poured tears, his lungs were clamoring for air.

Scott grabbed for the knife, or where he thought the knife should be, but his fingers closed on grass. He searched in a small circle, certain he had the right spot, but it wasn't there.

Desperate, Scott probed madly, running his hand back and forth. Pain seared his torso, pain from a biting flame. His flesh felt fit to explode. Weakness afflicted him due to the terrible heat, and he sagged, thinking his end had come.

"Pa! Where are you? Don't die! Please!"

Vail Marie's plaintive bawl did more than any gust of wind ever could. Marshaling his strength, Scott surged upward one more time, throwing himself against the wood like a living battering ram. Excruciating heat buffeted him. Flames danced before his eyes, even as red and orange claws sizzled at contact with his skin.

Abruptly, the wood gave way, spilling backward, sweeping most of the flames with it. The majority of the branches were now on his legs. Unless he extricated himself immediately, they would be burned to the marrow.

Scott had to take a breath. He couldn't hold air in any longer. Exhaling, he lowered his mouth to the ground where the smoke wasn't as thick. But it still made him sputter and hack.

Gripping the second stake, Scott tugged. The Indians

had embedded it deep. More than one person was needed to pull it out. But Nate was gone, and the Utes had their hands full staying alive.

Scott was on his own. It was do or die. Filling his mind with an image of Lisa and Vail Marie, he wrapped his hand around the stake, bunched his shoulders, and propelled himself upward.

The stake still wouldn't budge.

Nate King slowed within two bounds of leaving the clearing. The tall warrior had seemingly vanished like a ghost. Or had dropped down low and was waiting for someone to come within reach of his knife.

Palming his second pistol, Nate slunk into a cluster of cottonwoods that bordered the stream. A heel mark showed he had guessed correctly.

From the clearing rose lusty shouts, wavering screams, and a child's screams. The crack of a twig was almost drowned out. Nate spun, just as a knife flashed at his neck. By a sheer fluke the flintlock was rising and the knife smashed against it. Nate leaped to the right to gain room to shoot, but the tall warrior was on him like a wolf on a ram, the cold steel glittering as it weaved an invisible tapestry.

Nate was given no chance to use the pistol, exactly as the tall warrior planned. The knife never slowed, never gave him an opening. Constantly retreating, Nate backed into cottonwood after cottonwood.

Without warning, Nate's heel slipped on an incline. He had reached the bank. Seeking to throw himself to the left, he felt his foot lose traction on the slick ground. Down he went, the tall warrior on him before he could rise higher than one knee.

Steel *spang*ed off steel. A foot slammed into Nate's chest and he was knocked into the water. The man attacked again, a two-legged wolverine who wouldn't relent until his quarry was lifeless.

Flat on his back, water rushing past his ears, Nate

evaded a jab at his throat. He shoved the pistol's muzzle against his foe's ribs and fired, but it had gone under when he fell and all he heard was a dull click.

The tall warrior sprang back, then grinned wickedly as he realized the gun was useless. With renewed ferocity he waded in, delivering a flurry of strikes, slashes, stabs. Nate defended himself as best he was able, deflecting some with the pistol, dodging and ducking others, and all the while retreating in the face of the onslaught. He bumped into the opposite bank and shifted as the blade lanced at his heart. Hurling the flintlock at the warrior, he rotated and scrambled to the top before the man could recover and sink icy steel into his back.

Nate looked for a limb to use as a club and spied a suitable branch, but the warrior pounced before he could reach it. Weaving, skipping right and left, he avoided swings that would have reduced him to ribbons. The longer it went on, the more reckless the warrior became. He pressed Nate relentlessly, the blade always in motion, slicing, hacking, cleaving.

Their clash carried them in among pines. Slipping behind a broad trunk, Nate kept it between them, going right when the warrior did and left when his foe reversed direction. The warrior grew more and more angry, overextending himself when he lunged.

It was the moment Nate had waited for, the moment he had gambled he would live long enough to exploit. For although he had left the Hawken beside the pyre and both pistols were spent, he still had his long knife in its beaded sheath on his hip. He'd made no attempt to draw it, and in the swirl of frantic battle Nate figured the tall warrior had forgotten it was there. If the man had ever noticed it at all.

Now, as the warrior came at him from the left, Nate glided backward around the bole, luring the man after him. Nate waited for the warrior to lunge, for when he was off balance and his chest was exposed. That was when Nate's hand swept up and out, clasping the Green

River knife. The long blade was close to the pine, so the warrior wouldn't see it until too late.

In his fury at being foiled, the man uttered a vicious snarl. It changed to a startled grunt, then a gurgling groan, and he looked down at the weapon buried to the hilt between his ribs. Surprise widened his eyes. Grabbing it, he yanked the blade out. With it came a scarlet geyser, a fountain that turned the soil underfoot bright red.

Nate was crouched low in case the warrior came at him again. It was well he did, because the man howled and did just that, raining blow after blow. Nate retreated, losing the shelter of the pine. He went fifteen feet, but no farther.

There was no need. The tall warrior had stopped short and was gasping like a fish out of water. From his abdomen down he was caked crimson. Staggering, he stared at Nate and said something in his own tongue.

"Just die," Nate responded.

The man obliged. Legs turned to wax, he oozed to the ground and lay on his side, blank eyes fixed on the one who had slain him.

Straightening, Nate exhaled and hastened to reclaim his knife and pistol. That done, he jogged toward the clearing.

The sounds of battle had died.

Uncertain who had won, Nate approached cautiously. As he stepped into the clearing, the first sight to greet him was that of Swift Elk, bloodied but victorious, taking the scalp of the enemy he'd defeated.

All the enemy warriors were dead. Two of the Utes, as well, with a third severely wounded.

The fire still burned, although most of the wood had been scattered widely about as if by an explosion. The right-hand stake had been ripped from the earth and broken in half.

Several blazing brands were near the Hawken. Nate

wiped the rifle off, then faced the deliriously happy trio at the clearing's edge.

Scott Kendall had never been happier in his life. Tears of joy flowed over his ruddy cheeks as he hugged his darling wife and sweet daughter close. No words were spoken. None were needed.

Nate walked over, slowing when Swift Elk rose, beaming, and proudly waved the grisly trophy. "Your father will be proud," Nate signed.

"I am proud," the young warrior said in Ute, "to call Grizzly Killer my friend."

Scott and Lisa were still locked in a tender embrace, but Vail Marie had stepped back and put her hands on her hips. "I think their mouths are locked together, Uncle Nate," she commented as he stopped.

"It's called being in love."

"Have you ever kissed Aunt Winona like that?"

"Not often enough, I think."

"Everything is all right now, isn't it? We're safe, aren't we?"

"Everything is fine," Nate said, lifting the girl into his arms. "Let's leave your ma and pa alone awhile. What would you like to do?"

"Are you any good at pulling trees out of the ground?"

"How's that again?"

"Samson and Pa can do it. I bet you can, too, if you try real hard."

Nate King's laughter rolled off across the woodland, and in the trees a robin began to warble merrily.